Hearts
in
Darkness

NEW YORK TIMES BESTSELLING AUTHOR
LAURA KAYE

Hearts in Darkness
SECOND EDITION May 2013 by Laura Kaye
FIRST EDITION April 2011
HEARTS IN DARKNESS © Laura Kaye.
ALL RIGHTS RESERVED.

ISBN 978-0-9894650-0-7

Front Cover Art by Tricia "Pickyme" Schmitt
Back Cover and Interior by The Killion Group

PRAISE FOR HEARTS IN DARKNESS

"Get ready for a unique tale that will have you swooning for this very unusual hero!" ~RT Book Reviews

"It's been quite a long time, if ever, that I've read sex scenes that were just as emotionally moving as they were physically passionate....a truly spectacular reading experience that just made me hungry for more of Laura Kaye's work." ~One Good Book Deserves Another

"Wow! What an absolutely incredible little book to read! Such a beautiful story. I HIGHLY RECOMMEND IT! 'A 2011 Top Ten'!" ~Smitten with Reading

"A hot, sweet, and captivating short story that I am calling a must read." ~Book Savvy Babe

TITLES BY LAURA KAYE

Heroes Series
(Contemporary military romance)
HER FORBIDDEN HERO
ONE NIGHT WITH A HERO

Hard Ink Series
(Contemporary military romance)
HARD AS IT GETS, 11/26/13
HARD AS YOU CAN, 2/25/14

Hearts of the Anemoi Series
(Paranormal romance)
NORTH OF NEED
WEST OF WANT
SOUTH OF SURRENDER
EAST OF ECSTASY, 4/2014

Vampire Warrior Kings Series
(Paranormal romance)
IN THE SERVICE OF THE KING
SEDUCED BY THE VAMPIRE KING
TAKEN BY THE VAMPIRE KING, 8/1/13

Single Titles
FOREVER FREED
 (Paranormal romance)

JUST GOTTA SAY
(Contemporary erotic romance)

Love looks not with the eyes, but with the mind;
and therefore is winged Cupid painted blind.

~William Shakespeare

DEDICATION

To Lea, My Soul Sister

And to all the readers who have loved Caden and Makenna

CHAPTER ONE

"Wait! Can you please hold that?"

Makenna James huffed her frustration at her crappy day as she jogged toward the waiting elevator. Her cell phone rang in her suit jacket pocket. She shifted her bags over her right shoulder to pull it out. The bleating ring tone was as annoying as an alarm clock in the morning, but it was probably just that the damn thing hadn't stopped ringing all afternoon.

She glanced up just long enough to glimpse a big tattooed hand holding the elevator door open as she finally freed the small black phone. She spun it around in her hand to answer it and fumbled, sending it crashing and skidding along the dull marble floor.

"Shit!" she muttered, already fantasizing about the bottle of wine she was going to demolish once she got home. At least the phone skittered toward the still-waiting elevator. God bless the patience of the Good Samaritan holding it.

Makenna bent down to retrieve the phone, then stumbled into the elevator. Her long hair swung into her face, but she didn't have a free hand to push it back.

"Thanks," she mumbled to the Good Samaritan as her laptop strap fell off her shoulder bringing her purse with it to the floor. The elevator beeped its impatience even as the man removed his hand and the doors eased shut.

"No problem" came a deep voice from behind her. "What floor?"

"Oh, um, lobby, please."

Distracted by her purse and the day in general, Makenna hiked her laptop strap higher on her shoulder, then reached down to grab her purse. She slung it over her arm once more and looked down at her phone to see whose call she'd missed. The LED screen was black.

"What the…?" She flipped the phone around and found a gaping rectangular hole where the battery should be. "That's just perfect."

There was no way Makenna could be without her phone. Not with her boss calling every five minutes to check on the progress of her work. That it was Friday night and the beginning of the weekend made little difference to him toward the end of a project. She'd be glad when this contract was up.

With a sigh, she reached a tired hand over to the panel and jabbed at the button to return to the sixth floor. From the corner of her eye, she glimpsed just how tall her Good Samaritan was.

Then the elevator jolted to a stop and everything went pitch black.

ᴥᴥᴥ

Caden Grayson tried not to chuckle at the frazzled redhead careening towards the elevator. Why did women carry so many bags anyway? If it didn't fit in the pockets of his worn-soft jeans, he didn't carry it.

As the woman reached down to scoop up her phone—another thing Caden refused to carry unless he was on call—he found himself mesmerized by the way her hair tumbled over her shoulder in a long waterfall of soft, wavy red.

When the woman finally made it into the elevator, she murmured distractedly that she was going to the lobby too. He stepped back against the rear wall and bowed his head as he always did. He didn't really care if people stared at his piercings and ink, but that didn't mean he went out of his way to see their looks of disapproval or, worse, fear.

Caden shook his head in amusement as the woman continued to juggle her belongings and spat out a string of expletives under her breath. His day had been a complete pisser, so he was almost ready to join in with her—though his particular coping mechanism usually had him looking for the humor in a situation. And he found Red damn funny. He was grateful for the distraction.

Red reached in front of him to press a button. Caden almost laughed when she punched it at least five times. But the laughter died in his throat when he caught the scent of her shampoo. One of the things he loved about women: their hair *always* smelled like flowers. And that scent, combined with the redness and the softness and the waviness...Caden shoved his hands in his jeans pockets to keep from running his fingers through the thick mass of her hair. But, Christ, how he wanted to, just once.

And then Red disappeared, along with everything else, as the elevator jerked to a stop and the lights went out.

Caden gasped and stumbled back into the corner of the elevator. Clenching his eyes, he lowered his head into his hands and counted backwards from ten, trying to remember his breathing techniques, trying to keep from flipping the fuck out.

The confined space of the elevator was one thing—years of therapy had gotten him past that. Mostly. But confined spaces with no lights? No way. The pounding of his heart and tightness in his chest told him that was a complete fucking deal breaker.

He was on five when he realized Red was making a noise. He managed to push through his fear enough to hear she was laughing. Hysterically.

Caden opened his eyes, though they were useless. But he could tell from Red's laughter she was still near the bank of call buttons. And, amazingly, the more he focused on her, the faster his panic receded—or, at least, it didn't worsen.

God, he wished he could see her. He could almost imagine her shoulders shaking and her eyes tearing and her clutching her stomach from the force of her now breath-stealing laughter. When she snorted, Caden quirked a grin, as her less-than-graceful noises set her off to laughing once more.

But he didn't mind, because he found himself standing upright again, breathing more normally. He'd beaten back the panic. Thanks to her.

♥♥♥

Makenna would've shouted if she could've, but she was laughing so hard she could barely breathe. *Perfect! This is just freaking perfect!*

Nobody would believe the big steaming pile of crap her day had been. It started when she broke the heel on her favorite pair of strappy sandals walking up the stairs out of the metro. She'd had to turn around and make the twenty-minute trip back to her apartment to change shoes, simultaneously making herself late for work and earning herself blisters on both pinky toes from choosing the only other shoes—a pair of new heels—that matched her suit. It had all gone downhill after that. And now this. It was like...some stupid sitcom. With canned laughter and all. She snorted at the thought. The ridiculousness of the sound and the situation and her whole blasted day had her laughing again until her right side cramped and her cheeks burned from how wide she was smiling.

Finally, she dropped her bags somewhere on the floor next to her and reached out a hand until she encountered a cold metal wall. Bracing herself as she tried to calm down, she used her free hand to wipe away tears and fan the heat crawling up her face as she remembered Good Sam was in there with her.

Oh God. He probably thinks I'm a complete lunatic.

"Sorry, sorry," she finally choked out as the laughs turned into occasional chuckles. Now she was laughing at herself.

Good Sam didn't reply.

"Hello? You still with me?"

"Yeah, I'm here. You okay?" His voice resonated in the confined space, surrounded her.

"Um, yeah. I have no idea." She brushed her hair back off her face and shook her head.

The low sound of his chuckle made her feel a little less ridiculous. "That bad, huh?"

"The worst," Makenna said and sighed. "How long do you think we'll be in here?"

"Who knows. Hopefully not long." His voice had an edge to it Makenna didn't understand.

"Yeah. Don't these things usually have emergency lights?" She ran her fingers over the bank of call buttons and randomly pushed some looking for the alarm button, but none of them seemed to do anything. And she knew from working in this building for the past two years that the receiver was missing from the emergency phone cord. The hazards of working in a 1960s-era office building, apparently.

"The newer ones do."

Makenna finally gave up on the buttons. She turned towards the door and rapped her knuckles against the metal three times. "Hey! Anybody there? Can anyone hear me? We're stuck in the elevator." She pressed her ear against the cool surface of the doors, but after several minutes it was clear no one had heard. Makenna bet the elevator stopped somewhere between the third and fourth floors, which housed satellite offices of the Social Security Administration. The agency closed at five and was a ghost town by quarter after. It would certainly explain the lack of response.

Sighing, she held her hand up, but couldn't see it, even when her palm got close enough to touch her nose. "Damn, this is the very definition of pitch black. I can't even see my hand in front of my face."

Good Sam groaned. Makenna dropped her hand. "What?"

"Nothing." His voice was clipped, tight.

Oookay.

He huffed out a breath and moved around. Makenna yelped in surprise when something hard crashed into her ankle.

"Damn, I'm sorry. Are you okay?"

Makenna reached down and rubbed where his shoe, apparently, had kicked her. "Yeah. Did you sit down?"

"Yeah. Might as well get comfortable. I really didn't mean to kick you though. I didn't realize…"

"What? You couldn't see me standing here?" She laughed, trying to make light of their situation and break the ice a little, but his lack of reply rang loudly in the small space.

Makenna sighed and used her hand to guide her way back over to "her side" of the elevator. She tripped when her left foot got caught in the strap of one of her bags. Her heel slipped off. She kicked the other one off in defeat. It tumbled…somewhere into the darkness.

"I guess I might as well get comfortable, too, then," she said, as much to fill the dark silence as to make small talk with him. She found the back corner of the elevator and sat down, then carefully stretched her legs out in front of her and crossed her ankles. She smoothed her skirt over her thighs and then rolled her eyes at her actions. It wasn't like he could get a peek right now anyway.

The darkness was so disorienting. Not a hint of ambient light filtered in anywhere. Her impulse was to use the LED on her cell phone to shed some bluish light on their predicament, but its battery was currently somewhere in the elevator lobby of her floor. And, because this day was what it was, she'd drained the battery to her laptop earlier, so it wasn't any use either.

She wished she knew what Good Sam looked like. His aftershave was clean scented. She bit back a laugh as the thought of running her nose up his throat dashed through her head.

Makenna couldn't tell how much time was passing. She twiddled her thumbs, counting to a hundred twiddles as she also shook her ankles back and forth.

Why isn't he saying anything? Maybe he's shy. Or maybe you shocked and awed him with your graceful entrance, elegant nervous breakdown, and sexy snorting. Yeah, that must be it.

Caden wished Red would laugh again, or at least talk. Her reminders about just how goddamned dark it was in this suffocating box of an elevator had quickly reawakened his anxiety. When the tightness settled back into his chest, he'd sat down so he didn't embarrass himself by passing out or some shit and kicked her when he'd stretched out his legs. She hadn't uttered more than two sentences since.

Good going, man.

He heard her over there fidgeting and sighing and shifting. He started concentrating on the sound of her legs shaking against the short-knapped carpet of the elevator floor, and the distraction helped him slow his breathing. The deep breath he finally pulled into his lungs relieved and surprised him.

Caden was kind of a loner. He had a few close friends— people who'd known him most of his life and knew what happened when he was fourteen—but otherwise he didn't spend much time talking to people he didn't know. Part of that he did himself. The ink and the piercings and the skull trim all gave off an antisocial vibe, even if that was more image than reality. So it was odd for him to siphon calmness off another person the way he was doing with Red. He didn't even know what she looked like, for God's sake, or what her name was.

There was one way to fix that. "Hey, Red?" His voice sounded loud in the small space after the long moments of quiet. "What's your name?" he asked in a quieter voice.

She cleared her throat. "Everyone calls me M.J. You?"

"Caden. Is M.J. your name, or just what everyone calls you?"

She chuckled. "Well, *Caden*"—her emphasis on his name brought an unexpected smile to his face—"my name is Makenna, but M.J. seems to have stuck."

"What's the J for?"

"My last name is James."

"Makenna James," he whispered. He liked the name. It fit all that thick, luscious red hair. "You should go by Makenna. It suits you." Caden grimaced as he waited for her reaction to his unsolicited opinion. His mouth had worked faster than his brain.

"Hmm," she replied noncommittally. He thought he'd offended her until she continued, "Well, one advantage of M.J. is it doesn't make me stand out in my firm."

"What do you mean?"

"I'm the only woman."

"What do you do?"

"Are we playing Twenty Questions now?"

He grinned. He liked a woman who gave as good as she got. For an instant, the darkness felt almost freeing—she wouldn't be able to judge his appearance. And he was enjoying her openness. "Why not?"

She laughed softly. "Well, in that case, I've answered a lot more than you. What's your last name?"

"Grayson. Caden Grayson."

"And what do *you* do, Mr. Grayson?"

He swallowed thickly at the sound of her saying his name that way. It…did things to him. "Um"—he cleared his throat—"I'm a paramedic." Caden had known what he wanted to be since he was a teenager. It wasn't easy seeing other people, other families, in situations like the one that'd changed his life, but he'd felt called to do it.

"Wow. That's great. Very impressive."

"Yeah. It pays the bills," Caden said, embarrassed at the compliment. He wasn't used to receiving them. As he thought, he brushed a hand back and forth against the short-trimmed hairs on the top of his head. His fingers trailed over his most prominent scar. "How about you?" When she chuckled, he wondered what amused her.

"I'm an accountant, and, before you die of boredom over there, I do forensic accounting, so it's not as bad as it sounds."

He found himself laughing, though he wasn't sure why. Something about her just made him feel good. "Well, that's very...interesting."

"Shut up." She chuckled again.

He grinned broadly. "Good comeback."

She huffed and her voice sounded amused. "If I could see you, I'd smack you."

The sudden reference to the darkness chased the smile from his face. He gulped down a deep breath through his constricting throat.

"Hey, where'd you go?"

"Nowhere." He couldn't help the shortness in his tone, though his frustration was more at himself than her. He didn't like losing his shit, certainly not in front of other people.

"I'm sorry. Um...I wouldn't really hit you, you know."

Just like that, she refocused him. "Oh, well, I feel better now," he said, amusement threading back into his voice. And it was true. He rolled his head on his shoulders and released some of the tension in his neck. She was quiet for a while, making him wonder if she really thought he'd been upset about her comment. He didn't like the idea she might be feeling badly. "Um, I'm a little claustrophobic is all. So, if you could, maybe, stop mentioning it's dark in here, even though...shit."

"What?"

"Well, obviously it's dark, but I can avoid thinking about how tight and...close it is in here when you're talking— just, talk about something else." He rubbed his hand roughly over his skull trim knowing he sounded like a complete idiot, which was why he didn't often get to know anyone beyond his small circle.

But her reply sounded completely earnest. "Oh, okay. Well, then, what should I talk about?"

CHAPTER TWO

"Hell, I don't know. How about that game of Twenty Questions?"

Makenna smiled at his gruffness but couldn't blame him. She'd be freaking out if she were claustrophobic and thought he had to be strong to sit there so calmly. She wondered if that was why he'd been so quiet earlier and decided to help him through their hopefully temporary confinement.

"Okay. You go first."

"Okay." He was quiet for a moment, then said, "What's a forensic accountant?"

"An accountant who analyzes accounting and business practices as part of an investigation, like for litigation."

"Oh, well, that actually does sound interesting. Like detective work."

She appreciated his effort, but was so used to people developing narcolepsy at the mere mention of being an accountant that she wasn't sure if he was being serious. "Are you making fun of me?"

"Not at all," he replied. The speed of his words confirmed his sincerity.

"Okay, then. My turn?"

"Fire away."

Makenna smiled. "Did I see a tattoo on your hand?"

He didn't answer right away. "Yeah. It's the head of a dragon."

Makenna didn't have any tattoos—she'd been afraid it would hurt to get one—but she'd also always been a little fascinated by them. "Is it just the head?"

"Hey, it's my turn now."

"That wasn't a new question," she argued, "that was simply a clarification of my previous question."

"I thought you were an accountant, not a lawyer." He chuckled. "Fine. The whole dragon's on my arm and its head's on the back of my hand. Now, is it my turn, counselor?"

Makenna couldn't help but smile at his sarcasm. Growing up with three brothers had taught her the fine art of banter. "You may proceed."

He laughed and she liked the ring of it. "How very magnanimous of you."

"Ooh, pulling out the SAT words now, are we?"

"What? A guy with a tattoo can't use a four-syllable word?"

Makenna sucked in a breath, then sighed. "I wish I could see your face so I could tell if you're being serious or not." Then, just in case her indirect reference to the darkness bothered him, she hurried to add, "That's *so* not what I was saying. Just yanking your chain. It's your turn, already."

His low chuckle made her smile in relief. "Yeah, yeah. Okay. What made a girl like you become an accountant?"

A girl like me?

"A girl like me?" Makenna frowned and awaited his explanation. She couldn't begin to fathom what he meant.

"Just..." Caden sighed and murmured something she couldn't understand. "You're pretty."

Makenna went from flattered to perturbed and back again. In the end, she couldn't decide which emotion to settle on. Growing up in a houseful of boys turned her into a tomboy from as early as she could remember. Although her college roommates introduced her to girly things like dresses and skirts and lingerie and makeup, she still thought of herself as just one of the guys. Nothing remarkable. Certainly not the kind of girl her brothers drooled over.

"Um, shit, that didn't come out right either. I mean, you *are* pretty, but of course pretty girls can be smart. I mean— shit, I'm just gonna stop talking now."

Makenna finally settled on amused and burst out laughing. "Yes, now would be a good time to put down that shovel." Getting more serious, she said, "Well, and this will no doubt up my geek factor to you, but I was always very good at math, and numbers just came easy to me. I didn't really want to go into the theoretical side of it and teach. And then my oldest brother became a cop. He told me about forensic accounting."

Caden didn't respond, and Makenna was almost certain she'd put him to sleep. Then he said, quietly, "I really like the sound of your voice."

Makenna's flush ran down into the neck of her silk blouse. Saying she was pretty hadn't gotten to her, but his saying he liked her voice set butterflies loose in her stomach.

"Me, too. I mean, I like it, too. Your voice, that is." Makenna bit her lip to cut off the spectacular stream of nonsense coming out of her mouth, then pretended to thunk herself in the forehead. In that moment, she was glad for the darkness.

❧❧❧❧

Caden felt lucky Makenna was as easygoing as she was, because if he put his foot in his mouth one more time, he was sure she'd make good on her threat to smack him. First, he jumped to conclusions, assuming she'd judged him when she learned of his tattoo. He'd just been so disappointed she might disapprove of him even without seeing him. Then, his verbal filter failed, and he'd called her pretty. He'd been thinking of her red hair again and, without a doubt, it was pretty, beautiful even, but it slipped out without him thinking about the caveman way he'd phrased the question. And then he'd actually admitted he liked her voice. It was true, but he didn't need to be saying that shit out loud.

But then she'd said it too. And the dynamic shifted back in his favor. She'd stumbled over her own compliment. He thought maybe, just maybe, she enjoyed him saying he liked her voice.

He searched his mind to think of another question, one that ran less risk of him encountering bodily harm at her hand. He finally came up with "How many brothers do you have?" He probably should've thought of something else, but the words were out of his mouth.

Her voice sounded like she was smiling. "Three. Patrick's the oldest. He's the one who became a cop. Ian's next. And Collin's a year younger than me. Do you have any siblings?"

"His name was Sean. He was two years younger than me." Caden waited, suspecting Makenna would pick up on his use of the past tense.

Finally, her response came. "I'm sorry. I can't imagine losing one of my brothers. That must've been very hard. Can I ask how long ago he…you lost him?"

Something about the darkness made it safe to share some of this story. She couldn't see his grimace or the ticking of his clenched jaw. She couldn't wonder about the way he flexed his right shoulder so he could feel the skin over his shoulder blade move where Sean's name was inked. And she couldn't see the crescent-shaped scar on the right side of his head he always fingered when he got tangled in memories of his brother.

"I'm sorry. You don't have to talk about it."

"Don't apologize. I don't talk about him often, but maybe I should. He died when I was fourteen. He was twelve. That was fourteen years ago." As he said the words, Caden could hardly believe he'd been alive longer without Sean than he'd been with him. He'd been the best friend Caden ever had.

◦◦◦◦◦◦

Makenna burned to reach out to him. She shoved her hands flat under her thighs to keep from seeking out a hand to hold or a shoulder to squeeze. She didn't know this man from Adam, but she hurt for him. Two years ago when Patrick had been shot in the line of duty, she'd experienced a kind of terror she never wanted to feel again. And she could only imagine the way that feeling would've been amplified if her brother hadn't pulled through. She could hear it in Caden's voice.

But she couldn't resist some small gesture, so she said, "Thanks for sharing that, Caden. That's so damn young. I'm really sorry."

"Thanks" came his whispered reply. "So"—he cleared his throat—"how old are you?"

Makenna figured he'd appreciate her lightening things up, so she said in her most haughty voice, "Why, Mr. Grayson, what kind of question is that to ask a lady?"

"You're fascinated with numbers, so I'd think you'd be happy to tell me about this one."

She smiled as the good humor returned to his voice. "Fine." She exaggerated a sigh. "I'm twenty-five."

"A mere babe."

"Shut up, old man."

He barked out a laugh that made her grin.

A comfortable silence enveloped them. But now, without the conversation to distract her, Makenna was hot. It might've been the end of September, but the daytime temperature still felt like the middle of the summer. The lack of air conditioning was starting to make a difference inside the old elevator and her silk blouse clung uncomfortably.

Makenna shifted up onto her knees and shrugged out of her suit jacket. She folded it as neatly as she could and tossed it gently in the general direction of her bags.

"What are you doing?" Caden asked.

"Taking off my jacket. I'm getting a little warm. I wonder how long it's been." She untucked her blouse and shook the hem to fan air onto her abdomen.

"I don't know. Maybe an hour, hour and a half?"

"Yeah," Makenna agreed, figuring it was somewhere around 8 p.m. Someone would surely figure out they were in here sooner or later, right? Sighing, she settled back into her corner, but turned on her hip a little. Even though it was carpeted, the floor was hard. Her behind was falling asleep. "So, whose turn is it?" she asked.

Caden chuckled. "No idea. You can go though."

"What big plans did you have for tonight?"

"No big plans, really. I was just going to meet some buddies to play pool. I work a lot of night shifts, so I don't get to hang out with them as much as I'd like."

Makenna thought that sounded nice. Except for her college friends, only one of whom was in the D.C. area with her, she didn't have many girl friends to hang out with. For some reason, she'd always had an easier time making guy friends. She blamed being surrounded by her brothers and all their friends growing up.

"How 'bout you?"

"Oh, I had a very important date with my couch and a bottle of wine."

"I'm sure they'll reschedule."

"Yeah." Makenna chuckled, then sighed. "They're pretty much always available. Okay...moving on from that depressing topic..."

"Are you seeing anyone?" Caden asked, *not* getting off the depressing topic at all.

"Obviously not. You?"

"No."

Makenna took more pleasure in his answer than she thought she should. Maybe she was just happy she wasn't the only single person left out there. All her friends seemed to either be getting married or engaged. It was like a line of dominos falling, only she didn't seem to be in line.

"Okay," Caden said with a clapping sound that rang loud in the small space, "favorite color."

"Seriously?"

"Down to basics, Red."

She smiled widely at the nickname so many others had called her but she'd never really liked until now.

"Blue. Yours?"

"Black."

She smirked. "How very boy of you."

He chuckled. And launched into at least another twenty questions of the kind of minutiae you learned about a person after a couple months of dating: favorite band, favorite movie, favorite food, favorite place, favorite-everything-else-he-could-think-of, most embarrassing moment, and best day ever, though he skipped asking about worst day ever. Makenna was glad—she didn't think she could resist touching him if he talked about his brother again.

Makenna enjoyed the conversation. Some time in the middle of discussing favorites, she stretched out on the floor and propped herself up on her elbow. Despite being trapped in a pitch black elevator for a couple hours with a stranger, she felt surprisingly relaxed. The smallest niggling thought snuck into the back of her mind—she was kind of not looking forward to when the power came back on and they'd go their separate ways.

And, even more than that, they had a surprising amount in common. They both loved Italian and Thai food. She could even overlook his love of sushi since he was such a huge fan of Kings of Leon, her absolute favorite band. They both enjoyed going to baseball games, mostly to sit out in the sun and drink beer with friends, and neither understood the point of golf at all. And they shared a love for stupid humor movies, even though they couldn't agree on ranking them.

It was the most entertaining conversation Makenna had had in a very long time. Caden seemed genuinely interested in her answers. And he debated and argued every little point in a way that made her want to kiss him to shut him up. She liked the way she felt around this man, despite the fact she'd never laid eyes on him.

～～～

Caden couldn't remember the last time he'd had such an easy conversation or the last time he'd laughed or even smiled so much. It felt...good—which was remarkable. He tended to operate somewhere between "fine" and "pretty good" most days. And he'd long ago made peace with that.

It was worlds better than the abyss in which he'd spent most of his teenage years.

"I gotta stand up and stretch," he said out of nowhere.

"Yeah, I know. This floor leaves a little to be desired."

"At least it's carpeted and not marble or tile. Your legs would be cold if it was." Caden reached his arms over his head and twisted his torso back and forth while he remembered the way her little gray suit skirt hugged her shapely bottom. His spine cracked when he turned to the left.

"Cold might feel good right now."

Makenna was right. It had gone from that over-air-conditioned feeling most office buildings had in the summer to comfortable to warm. It wasn't hot yet, but it was heading in that direction.

As Caden settled back on the floor and tried to find a position that didn't aggravate the tingles in his ass and hips, Makenna reopened the questions. "So, I work in this building, but what landed you in this fine elevator today?"

"Settling my father's estate. His law partner's office is on the seventh floor."

"Oh, I'm sor—"

"Don't be. My father was a very unhappy man for a very long time. And we didn't get along. He's gotta be in a better place now. Anyway, I just had to sign some paperwork."

He just barely heard Makenna's soft "Oh."

"So," he said, wanting to move away from yet another depressing topic, "first times—who, when, where, how good."

"What?" Makenna choked out an incredulous laugh. "Uh, I think not."

"Why not? We've talked about just about everything else. I'll even go first."

Makenna was quiet for a minute and then started moving around. She sounded closer than she'd been.

"What are you doing?"

"I'm not entertaining the idea of talking about this until I've at least broken bread with you. And I'm starving over here."

He'd been trying to ignore his stomach for the past...hell, he didn't even know how long. But her mention of food had him salivating.

Makenna was muttering, "Come on, come on, where is it. Not that bag." She nearly startled him with her triumphant "Ha! All right, Mr. Grayson, would you prefer a granola bar or a little bag of trail mix?"

He grinned, not expecting her to share with him, and he certainly had no intention of asking her to. "No, no. All yours."

"Come on, you have to eat something. I've got two, so there's one for each of us. Since this is my building, it's kind of like you're my guest. So you get to pick—granola bar or trail mix." Caden could hear her shaking the bags as she continued to say in a sing-song voice, "Granola bar or trail mix, granola bar or trail mix."

He smiled. "Okay, I'll take the trail mix."

"Done. Um, here?"

The package crinkled against the carpet as Makenna slid it in his direction. He reached his hand out in search of it. When they finally met somewhere in the darkened middle, Caden dragged his hand over hers. It was small and soft. He surprised himself by thinking he wanted to keep holding her hand more than he wanted the food. She didn't pull away. They both laughed nervously.

"We'll have to share the water, though. I only have one bottle."

"How much stuff do you have in there?"

"Hey, don't be knocking my bags. Without them, we wouldn't be sharing this gourmet meal right now."

"Agreed. Sorry," he said as he threw back the first handful of nuts and raisins.

They ate in silence and the salt from the trail mix made him thirsty. He felt awkward asking, but the idea of the water tortured him. "Can I have a drink now?"

"Of course. Let me make sure the cap's on tight so it doesn't spill." They executed the mid-elevator hand-off. Caden smiled as they once again paused with their fingers touching before pulling away.

He unscrewed the lid and tilted the bottle to his lips. "Oh, God. That's good."

"I know. I didn't realize how thirsty I was until I took a sip."

"Thanks for sharing your stuff with me."

"Of course. What was I going to do? Sit here and eat in front of you? Come on, you know me better than that. Then again, maybe not."

Caden thought he did know her...or at least he was starting to. Every story she'd shared with him revealed some part of her character—and everything he'd learned told of a person who was friendly and compassionate and giving. "No, you were right the first time," he finally said. "I do."

The trail mix was gone too soon, but at least it took the edge off. They passed the water back and forth until it was almost gone, then Caden insisted Makenna take the last drink.

They sat in the heat of the dark elevator for several minutes before Caden finally gazed in her direction and said, "Don't think your little ploy with the snacks distracted me from the current question on the table."

"Not at all. But you said you'd go first."

CHAPTER THREE

Makenna shifted onto her back and stared at the invisible ceiling. She had a big goofy grin on her face because Caden was about to tell her about his first time, while she had absolutely no intention of sharing hers.

"Okay. I'll start then. I am, after all, a man of my word. My first time was with Mandy Marsden—"

"Mandy?" Makenna wrinkled her nose and smirked.

"Hey, telling a story over here. Keep the editorial comments to a minimum."

"Oh, right, sorry. Please continue." Her smile grew wider.

"As I was saying…my first time was with Mandy Marsden, on her parents' living room couch while they were asleep upstairs. I was sixteen and had no idea what the hell I was doing. I remember it as being nice, but I imagine Mandy might have been…underwhelmed."

Makenna found the chuckle in his voice at the end there so endearing. She liked a guy who could laugh at himself. *He must be pretty confident in bed now to share a story like that*—the thought made her even hotter than she already was. "Sounds very romantic," she managed.

"Who knows from romance when you're sixteen?"

"Well, that's true, I suppose. Did you at least buy her dinner beforehand?"

"Does pizza count?"

She couldn't help but laugh. Caden was adorable. "For a sixteen-year-old, sure. I'll give you a pass."

"How big of you. Okay, then, your turn, Red."

She didn't answer.

"Red?"

"Next question."

She heard him roll over. His voice sounded closer. "No way. We had a deal."

"Could the court reporter please read back the transcript to ascertain Miss James never agreed to tell this story?"

He scoffed. "Okay, I realize we've been in here for a while, but please tell me you're not losing your mind already."

"Not at all, just getting the facts straight."

"Come on. What's the big deal?"

She was almost glad she couldn't see him—if his eyes were anywhere near as persuasive as his voice, she'd be a goner. "Just...no," she said through a laugh at his pleading.

"It couldn't be any worse than mine."

"Nope."

"Red."

"No."

"M.J."

"Hey, that's Makenna to you, mister. And the answer's still no." Even though her initials didn't bother her in the rest of her life, there was something about the way her name rolled off his tongue she really liked. She didn't want him to treat her just like everybody else did, just like one of the guys.

"This must be some story. You realize you're building expectations here."

She groaned. "No, no, no, no."

"Tell me and I'll take you out for pizza. You can even pick the toppings." They were just joking around, but Caden found himself hoping she'd agree to the pizza, even if it didn't get the story out of her. He wanted the hell out of this box, but he wasn't at all looking forward to walking away from Makenna. Or, more likely, her walking away from him.

Makenna didn't respond right away. Caden wished he

could see the look on her face, the set of her eyes. "What color are your eyes?" he whispered, once again losing the filter between his brain and mouth.

"Blue," she whispered back. "And, yes."

"Yes, what?" Caden asked, distracted by the desire to reach out and touch her face. The whispering made their conversation feel intense, intimate. And all of a sudden his body roared to life. This time, though, his racing pulse and pounding heart were a result of arousal rather than panic.

"Yes, I'll have pizza with you. If you'll see a movie with me."

Caden imagined her words slipping over his body. He wished it was her small, soft hands instead. But he was happy she'd agreed to go out with him, and that she'd turned it into a full-on date. "Yeah. Pizza and a movie, then." He rubbed his hand over his hair as the dark concealed the smile reshaping his face.

"My first time was with Shane Cafferty," Makenna started, still whispering. "I was eighteen. It was two weeks after prom. We sorta dated all summer before we went off to different colleges. But, that night, we took a blanket out and laid it in front of the pitcher's mound on the high school baseball diamond. Oh, God, this is so embarrassing," she groaned.

"It is not, out with it." He was surprised she'd finally relented, but her opening up made him feel hopeful.

"He'd been on the high school baseball team. He was good—at baseball, I mean, God—anyway, taking a blanket out there at night was kind of our thing. The first time was sweet. Short"—she laughed—"but sweet. It got better, though."

"That's a good story. Much better than mine. Thanks for sharing. See, that wasn't hard."

She sighed. "No, I guess it wasn't." She paused for a few moments and then said, "You know, you have an unfair advantage over me. You saw me when I came into the elevator, but I was too distracted to see you."

"Yes." He smirked at her through the darkness. "I remember. But I didn't see your face either because your hair was in the way."

"What color are your hair and eyes?" She shifted while she spoke and her voice got a little closer.

Caden itched to reach a hand out and measure just how close she was. His senses told him she was within reach. The thought made his arm ache for the feel of her. "Both brown, although I don't have much hair to speak of."

"Wh...why?"

Laughter spilled out of him. It broke the quiet between them, but not the intensity. "I keep my head shaved."

"Why?"

"I like it that way." He wasn't ready to reveal all his oddities to her just yet, because he didn't want to scare her away. He was half contemplating taking out his facial piercings before she could see them, but decided, somehow, that felt dishonest.

"Like buzz-cut shaved or like baby's-bottom-soft bald?"

"Give me your hand," Caden offered. "You can feel for yourself."

꒰ꔛ꒰ꔛ꒰ꔛ

Makenna gulped down her excitement at finally getting to do what she'd been dying to do most of the night. Her sight gone, she longed for another way to make a more tangible connection to Caden. And between the sex talk—G-rated though it might've been, and the plans for a date, and the whispering, and the feeling his body was close to hers, Makenna's body was starting to vibrate with a heady sense of anticipation that made her stomach flutter and her breath come a little faster.

Still lying flat on her back, Makenna gingerly reached out her hands. "Where are you?"

"Right here." Caden caught her right hand in his, and Makenna gasped at the contact. His hand engulfed hers as he pulled it up to his head.

Makenna's pulse raced as she smoothed her hand over Caden's head. His hair was shaved so close it felt soft and ticklish as she rubbed her fingers over it. Long after it was necessary, Makenna continued to stroke his hair. She didn't want to stop touching him. And when he scooted his body a little closer so she didn't have to extend her arm so far, she smiled, thinking he liked it, too.

"Tell me something else," Makenna said in a low voice, no longer whispering, but speaking soft enough she didn't chase away whatever magic was working between them.

"Like what?"

"Like...why a dragon?"

"Hmm." He leaned his head into her hand. She smiled. When he finally started speaking, his words came in an unbroken stream. "The dragon's my fear. I put it on my arm to remind myself I've tamed it. We, uh, we were driving home from a vacation at the beach. It was a little two-lane country road, and it was late at night because me and Sean had bugged our parents to let us have all day Sunday on the beach."

Makenna sucked in a breath at the gravity of what he was sharing with her. Her hand paused against his head as she wondered if she should say something, or if she should just let him talk. She was surprised to feel his big warm palm press her hand against his head, and took that as a sign he wanted her to keep rubbing him. So she did.

"My father was a stickler for going the speed limit. He never cared if twenty cars lined up behind him, blowing their horns and flashing their lights. You could pass on these back roads on the straightaways. People did it all the time. By the time we were about an hour away from the beach, it was all the way dark. I didn't see what happened at the time, but I found out later that a tractor trailer passed us, but moved back in his lane too soon. My father swerved to avoid getting hit."

Makenna's eyes welled with tears in anticipation of where the story was headed.

"The next thing I knew, the car was upside down. Wedged in a big irrigation ditch at the edge of a field. The passenger side took the worst damage when the car rolled, the side Sean and my mom were sitting on. I was the only one still conscious after the accident. But I couldn't move because a lot of our stuff from the back of the car—it was a station wagon, of all things—had tumbled forward into the back seat and buried me. My shoulder was dislocated, and I couldn't manage the leverage to dig myself out. I kept calling their names. But none of them would wake up. I passed in and out of consciousness a few times. Every time I woke up, it was dark and I was still trapped. We were there for about four hours before another passing tractor trailer finally spotted the car top-down in the ditch and called for help. By the time they got us out, Mom and Sean were gone."

"Oh, my God, Caden." Makenna willed him to feel the comfort and peace she so badly wanted him to have. From what he'd said earlier, she hadn't realized he'd lost his mother, too. She truly wished that wasn't something else they had in common. "I'm so sorry. No wonder..."

He gently grabbed her hand and slid it around to his cheek. Makenna whimpered when she felt him press his face into her palm. To her, his gesture seemed brave. She admired his ability to ask for what he needed. His cheekbone felt prominent under her fingers and a light stubble pricked against her palm. She rubbed her thumb gently back and forth.

"When I finally got over the worst of the claustrophobia, I got the dragon. I wanted to be strong for Sean. And I wanted him to know I wasn't going to live my life in fear, when he couldn't live his at all."

Makenna was swimming in emotion. The grief she felt for him was palpable; it ran down her temples into her hairline and constricted her throat. Her desire to protect him—to make sure nothing hurt him, scared him, took from him, ever again—came out of nowhere, but she felt the kind of kinship with Caden she'd always felt with her brothers. It didn't matter that she could still count the amount of time she'd known him in minutes.

And, God, she wanted him. She wanted to pull him down on top of her. She longed to feel his weight settle on her body, his lips on hers, his hands in her hair and gliding over her skin. It had been eleven months since she'd last been with someone, and never had she felt this kind of a connection. Makenna wanted her hands on him, too. Now that she was touching him, she worried she wouldn't be able to stop.

"Don't stop talking to me, Makenna. I need your words. Your voice."

"I don't know what to say is all. I want to take away your hurt."

His cheek lifted into a smile under her hand. "Thank you. But sometimes I think I need it. It reminds me I'm alive. And it makes the good times feel that much better. Like right now, being here, with you."

CHAPTER FOUR

Between the lack of any visual reference, her soft hand stroking his hair over and over, and managing to share the story of his mother's and Sean's deaths without once coming close to panicking, Caden was almost dizzy with triumph. It was Makenna, it was all Makenna's doing. And he adored her for it. No one had ever gotten into the heart of him the way she had, and certainly never as fast.

Makenna's voice interrupted his thoughts. "You say the sweetest things, Caden Grayson. I swear."

Caden smiled against her hand, still holding his cheek, and finally chuckled.

"What's so funny?"

He shrugged, then remembered the body language would be lost on her. "Sweet isn't a word usually applied to me."

"Well, then, people don't know you."

He nodded. "Maybe so." Probably so. He'd be the first to admit he kept people away. He didn't like the feeling of burdening others with his baggage. Sometimes distance was easier than acting, or explaining.

"Definitely so," she replied.

Caden liked her argumentative nature. She was playful and feisty and had him talking and laughing more in the couple hours he'd known her than probably in the whole last month combined. With her, he'd never given distance a second thought.

Caden almost moaned when she slid her palm up his face and began stroking from his temple, back over his ear, and down to his neck. His mouth dropped open. His breathing picked up. He couldn't help but lean into her surprisingly sensual touch.

He closed his eyes for a moment and just gave in to the feeling of it. He could hear her breathing and didn't think he was imagining her breaths coming quicker, too. The possibility she might be longing for him the way he was longing for her all at once made him hard. He groaned low in his throat before he could stop himself.

"Makenna."

"Caden."

Was her voice filled with longing, or was that just wishful thinking? Surely he was projecting his desire onto her, right? He swallowed thickly and shifted his hips. His button fly was relaxed, but not enough to accommodate his hard-on without discomfort.

Then, her fingers exerted pressure against the back of his neck. But she continued on with the steady stroking, and he thought he must've imagined it. He just wasn't sure. He concentrated all his focus on the movement of her hand and...*I didn't imagine it that time, did I?* There it was again—her fingertips pulling him towards her.

Please let me not be imagining that.

He licked his lips and moved his head forward just an inch or two. God, he wanted to kiss her. His fingers itched to finally thread their way into all that red hair. His lips fell open in anticipation of claiming her mouth. He wanted to taste her. He wanted to feel her under him.

"Makenna," he rasped, a plea, a prayer.

"Yes, Caden, yes."

It was all the confirmation he needed.

He pushed himself across the carpet until his chest encountered her side. He slowly lowered his head so he didn't hurt her in his blind impatience. His mouth found a cheek first and he pressed his lips against the soft apple of it. She moaned and wrapped her arms around his broad shoulders. His right hand landed in a pile of silky curls, and the satisfaction he felt at finally touching her hair made him swallow hard.

"So soft," he murmured, meaning her hair and her skin and the mound of her breast pressing against his chest where he lay atop her.

Caden let out his own moan when her lips pressed against the skin in front of his ear. She exhaled roughly, and the rush of her breath over his skin brought goose bumps to his neck.

He trailed soft kisses across her cheek until he found her lips.

And then he couldn't go slow anymore.

And neither could she.

Caden groaned as his first kiss brought her full bottom lip into his mouth. Both hands found their way to her face, and he cupped his palms around her cheeks so he could guide their movement. Makenna's high-pitched moan accompanied her hands grasping at the back of his head and neck.

When her mouth fell open, Caden accepted the invitation like a starving man at a feast. He slipped his tongue into her sweet mouth and relished the tantalizing caresses their tongues traded. Makenna stroked his head and massaged his neck and gripped his shoulders. Caden pulled himself closer to her because, as much as it was, it just wasn't enough.

He needed to be closer. He needed more of her.

�◠◡◠◡◠◡

Makenna was floating in the pleasure Caden's touch brought. The darkness combined with the intensity of their connection made her feel like nothing else existed in the world. She'd never experienced this kind of passion before—at least, not from a kiss alone.

From the minute he murmured those sweet words about how good it felt to be with her, she knew she was going to have to kiss him. She needed to taste the mouth of the man who'd survived such tragedy, but managed to retain so much gentleness, so much sweetness. She thought they'd shared the most honest and enjoyable conversation of her life. She yearned for more, for a way to burn it into her memory for all time.

In her mind, Makenna was saying "Kiss me, kiss me, kiss me," but she wasn't as confident as Caden seemed to be about asking for what she needed. So she stroked his head and gently pulled at his neck. And the anticipation he might actually realize what she was suggesting had her shifting her thighs at the noticeable dampness on her panties. All of this, and she'd never seen him. At least, not with her eyes.

She gasped when the warm weight of his firm chest fell across her breast. His hand gripped long locks of her hair as his mouth pressed gently against her cheek. She couldn't hold back her moan at the goodness of finally feeling him like this. Needing more of him, she cradled his head, holding him to her, then slid her hands lower, reveling in the sculpted ridges of his broad shoulders and solid biceps.

Then his lips claimed hers. While Makenna loved the sweet butterfly kisses he'd traced over her cheekbone, her need to connect with him was too great to go slow. Her mouth fell open after their first kiss, and Caden didn't disappoint. He pulled more of his torso on top of hers and explored her wanton mouth with his tongue. Sometimes he thrust and sometimes she parried. Every movement caused her heart to slam against her rib cage and her body to tingle in anticipation.

When Caden pulled back and pressed smaller kisses on her lips, Makenna took the opportunity to pursue him this time. She grabbed the back of his head and lifted her own as she kissed his mouth and sucked on his bottom lip. She gasped when she felt something metal on the side of his mouth and was so turned on at the unexpectedness of it that she groaned and licked at it. His answering grunt reverberated into her lower stomach. His lips quirked into a quick smile as she lavished attention on what she finally realized was a piercing of some sort.

More of the puzzle that was Caden Grayson came together just then. Tattoo. Piercing. Buzz cut. He must look rough on the outside. But he was a big, sweet, considerate, sometimes vulnerable softy on the inside. And she wanted to get to know both sides a lot better.

It was impossible to know how long they kissed in the darkness—time seemed to lose all meaning. But Makenna was breathless and needy and wet by the time he ran kisses and nips down her jaw line to her ear and, from there, down her neck. His short whiskers left a trail of fire against her skin as he moved. She curled her legs toward him, needing to feel more of him pressed against more of her. The groan he let loose when she hiked her knee across the back of his thigh made her whimper and rock her hips against him.

He pulled himself closer and slid his knee between her legs, keeping her from twisting her back the way she'd been. Not that she'd really noticed. Caden sucked the small diamond stud piercing her ear lobe into his mouth as his right hand ghosted over her body and settled on the hip wrapped around him.

"Oh God, Caden."

His cheek drew into a smirk where it pressed against her own, but she didn't mind him smirking when he licked and kissed and sucked at her neck the way he was doing. She tilted her head to the side to open to him, and ran her hands back up to offer encouraging caresses to his neck and head.

That was when she felt it. The fingers on her left hand clearly traced what could only be a scar on the side of his head. She hesitated for less than a second, but he apparently sensed it because he pulled back just a little.

"I'll tell you all about it," he whispered against her neck, "I promise."

She inhaled a breath to respond when the elevator jolted and light exploded in the small space.

Makenna yelped and clenched her eyes shut. Caden grunted and buried his face in the crook of her neck. After hours of staring into blackness, the light was painful, blinding.

Makenna was frustrated with the timing of the lights, relieved they were on, but fearful about what would happen to her and Caden now that they were.

And then the elevator shuddered. They plunged back into darkness.

They both groaned again and curled around one another as they tried to adjust to the strobing effect the lights left behind their eyelids. Makenna went from being blinded to seeing a swirling kaleidoscope of disorienting red and yellow spots.

"Shit," Caden rasped.

Makenna stopped worrying about her strained eyes and paid attention to him again, only to realize his body had gone rigid above her. *Oh no.* "Caden?"

His only answer was a strangled groan low in his throat and his left hand clutching a little tighter at her shoulder.

She understood what was wrong. She might've only known this man for a handful of hours. She might not ever have seen him. But she knew him. And she knew he needed her.

"Hey, hey," she cooed to him as she stroked his hair. "It's okay."

He didn't relax at all, but she sensed he was listening to her, or trying to.

"I'm here. And we're okay. We're gonna be okay. You're not alone." *This time,* Makenna added to herself. She was mentally cursing that teasingly temporary return of the electricity, because it'd offered the most glaring reminder of the whole night that Caden was trapped in a small, pitch-black metal box. She found herself furious on Caden's behalf. As she continued to stroke him and offer occasional murmured reassurances, mentally she cursed the inventor of the elevator, the electric company, her meter reader, and, while she was at it, threw in a few choice words for Thomas Edison, too, because, well, Caden wouldn't be trapped in a tiny electrical conveyance if good old Tom hadn't gone and found a way to apply electrical theory. She wasn't too happy with Ben Franklin and that damned kite, either.

Caden's shoulders finally unbunched. He shuddered and

inhaled. Makenna let out a breath she didn't realize she'd been holding.

"I've got you, Good Sam," she said with a relieved smile.

He nodded infinitesimally, but they were so close that she felt it nonetheless.

"Come here," Makenna offered as she guided his head from where it'd been buried in her neck to her opposite shoulder so he could lie alongside her. She stretched to wrap her arms around him and was just barely able to clasp her fingers together as she held him.

⁓⁓⁓⁓⁓

The shock of the flashing light set off a panic attack so unexpected, Caden had a hard time breathing. The only thing that kept him from losing his shit entirely was the calming scent of Makenna's hair and neck.

He didn't need to wonder why the light had set him off. All at once he was sucked fourteen years into the past, hanging upside down with his head wedged between the front center console and passenger seat, buried in a pile of baggage and vacation souvenirs. Something sharp stabbed into his side, making it difficult to take a deep breath without worsening the sting of it. His head rang and throbbed. Something wet ran down into his hair. And his right shoulder sat entirely too close to his jaw to be natural. For the longest time, the darkness and silence was eerily complete. But then the full horror of his situation would be fully illuminated by a flash of light from a passing car.

The first time it happened, Caden had been filled with relief and used much of what energy he still had screaming, "In here! We're in here!"

But no help came.

Not many headlights went by as the hour had become so late, but with each one Caden had his faith raised and dashed, his battered body further buffeted against the rocks of pleading hope and terrified disappointment.

As he passed in and out of consciousness, those rare moments were even harder to bear, because it became difficult for him to distinguish reality from nightmare. By the time a passing tractor trailer finally stopped to help several hours later, Caden was so sure he wouldn't survive the crash he didn't answer when the driver called out to ask if anyone could hear him.

"God, Caden, that's horrible."

He frowned and unthinkingly shifted his head to look up at Makenna's still-hidden face. "What?" he asked, his voice a dry scrape.

"I said that was a horrible thing for you to have gone through. I'm so sorry."

With a start, he understood he'd said out loud what he only thought he'd been remembering. And yet, here was Makenna, still holding him, soothing him, accepting him completely despite his infuriating childish fear.

For fuck's sake, he ought to be the one comforting her through this ordeal.

He leaned his head back into the crook of her neck and breathed deeply. Without having seen more of Makenna than her gorgeous red hair and her tight little backside, Caden was sure he'd be able to pick her out of a crowd by her luscious scent alone.

As he relaxed more fully, something she'd said came back to him. "Why did you call me 'Good Sam'?"

She squeezed her arms around him. He could hear the smile in her voice when she spoke. "Before I knew your name, I was thinking of you as my Good Samaritan. For holding the elevator door." She chuckled. "I really needed something nice to happen to me today, and you being patient enough to wait earned you the nickname."

Caden smiled. That he'd done something to make her day better unleashed a warm satisfaction through his body, easing the tight strain of his muscles. "Whatever you say, Red."

"You know, I'm close enough to smack you now."

He chuffed out a laugh, releasing more of his anxiety. "Go ahead, I might like it." Second by second, he was feeling more like himself again, relaxed enough that his body started responding to his memory of their phenomenal kissing. Not to mention the way she was wrapped around him. When Makenna coughed out a laugh, Caden smiled wider that she didn't come up with a witty retort. He liked that his comment flustered her.

Caden swallowed thickly and wished they had more water. He was too warm and covered in a sheen of panic-induced sweat, though neither discomfort gave him the first thought of pulling away from Makenna's equally overheated body.

One of Makenna's hands left his shoulder just as he heard the unmistakable noise of a yawn.

"Tiring of your stranded-elevator company already?" Caden asked, but also worried it could be true, particularly once she saw him.

"Never," she said through the tail end of the yawn. "Sorry. It'd been a long day hours before I had the pleasure of meeting you. And the heat is making me sleepy. And you're comfortable," she added in a small, tentative voice.

"So are you." He squeezed with the arm lying across her torso and tucked his fingers under her back to keep his hold firm. "Close your eyes, Red." Caden thought he could surely fall asleep in this woman's arms, but hated the idea of missing even one of what he was sure would be too few remaining captive minutes with her.

"I don't really want to," she protested in a whispered voice.

"Why not?"

She didn't answer right away, but finally said, "Because I'm...enjoying you."

Caden hid his smile in her neck and reached forward to press a rainfall of kisses on her soft skin. He traced his nose up the slender column of her throat to her ear. "Me, too," he breathed, enjoying her shiver. He pressed a kiss against the shell of her ear and added, "I'm sorry, for earlier."

One of her hands felt its way up to his face, where she tenderly cupped the hard angle of his jaw. "Please don't be. I'm just glad to be here for you."

He laid his head back on her shoulder. "But I want to be here for you."

"You are." He grumbled and she squeezed her arm around him. "Make you a deal: I'll help you through your claustrophobia, and you can help me with spiders."

"Spiders?" He chuckled.

"Those things have *way* too many legs to be acceptable. Don't even get me started on centipedes."

"Deal." He laughed, but inside he was beaming because her proposition only made sense if they were going to spend time together outside this damn elevator. And he really wanted that.

Hopeful, Caden pulled his hand out from under her back and stroked her long hair, threading his fingers through it from scalp to curled ends. When his fingers would linger over her scalp, she'd make a noise like a satisfied purring kitten, encouraging him to pet her over and over again.

Finally, her body relaxed under his. She fell asleep. And then it was his turn to feel satisfied—satisfied that this woman who hardly knew him and had never seen him felt safe enough in his arms to give herself over to the vulnerability of sleep. It was a trust he vowed never to break.

CHAPTER FIVE

Makenna awakened slowly and begrudgingly emerged from her dream. She'd been lying on a beach, the heat of the summer sun beating down on her, and her arms and legs had been entangled with her lover. She could almost feel his weight covering her.

And then she was awake enough to realize at least part of what she'd dreamed was real. The night came back to her in a rush. The elevator. Caden. The kisses. She smiled into the darkness.

She couldn't guess how long she'd been asleep, but it was long enough that her back protested the hardness of the floor.

"Hey." Caden's voice was gruff, thick with sleep.

"Hey. Sorry if I woke you."

"Nah. I've been in and out of sleep."

"Oh." Makenna covered a yawn.

"You snore," Caden said after a minute.

"I do not!" At least, she didn't think she did. It'd been a long time since she'd slept with someone else. She covered her eyes and groaned. When Caden chuckled, Makenna dropped her hand, turning her face in the direction of his.

"No, you don't. I just wanted to get a rise out of you."

"You suck," Makenna said through her own chuckle.

Caden shifted forward and pressed his lips against her throat. His kiss turned to suction as he drew her skin into his mouth. She gasped. After a few seconds he let go. "I *can* suck," he murmured as he kissed her again.

Oh my.

Her mind flirted with something witty, but all she could get out was a whimper as he pulled his lips away.

Caden shifted them, pulling Makenna onto her side facing him. She groaned, but not in pleasure. Her back screamed in protest.

"Are you okay?"

"Yeah, it's just…my back is kinda sore. Do you mind if we sit up?"

"Course not."

Makenna regretted losing the feeling of Caden's body, but sitting up relieved her back so much she moaned.

"Come here," Caden said, his voice now more distant from her.

"Where are you?"

"In the corner…you can lean against me."

Makenna smiled at his thoughtfulness—and his continued desire to touch her—and she crawled on her hands and knees toward where she thought he might be. Her fingers fell on a shoe, and she worked her way up his jeans-clad leg as she crawled between his bent knees.

Her hand touched his thigh, and he groaned. She bit her lip and smiled.

Carefully, she turned herself around and settled her body back against the hard plane of his warm chest. She hesitated for just a moment, then allowed her head to fall back onto his shoulder. He nuzzled against her hair. She could've sworn she heard him sniff, which reminded her of her earlier errant thought about running her nose up his throat. Pleased she could finally do what she'd wanted, she turned her face towards him and swam in the tantalizing scents of crisp, clean aftershave and man.

When he wrapped his arms around her waist, she sighed, then covered his arms with hers.

"Better?" he asked.

"Mmm, much. Thanks."

She felt him nod and smiled when he pressed a kiss onto her hair. Being with Caden this way—sitting so close, in his arms, him kissing her—it was totally crazy. She knew it was. So why did it feel so right?

Makenna was tired, but didn't think she could sleep. It was stifling in the elevator. She suspected the heat was as responsible for her exhaustion as the hour.

"Got any more questions?" she asked after a while, wanting to hear his voice again.

Caden chuckled and his chest rumbled against her back. "Hmm...where do you live?"

"You know the shopping center at Clarendon, where the Barnes and Noble and Crate and Barrel are?"

"Yeah."

"I live in the apartments above that.

"Those are pretty new, aren't they?"

"Yeah, I've been there about a year. It's great for people watching. I sit on my balcony a lot and watch the kids run around the playground and the people walk between the shops. How 'bout you, where do you live?"

"I got a townhouse in Fairlington. I work out of the firehouse there, so it's pretty convenient. Does your family live around here, too?"

"No. My dad, Patrick, and Ian still live outside of Philadelphia, where I grew up. And Collin's in graduate school in Boston." Makenna hesitated for a moment, then said, "My mom died when I was three. Breast cancer."

Caden hugged her tighter. "Shit, I'm sorry, Makenna. I went on and on—"

"Stop, really. I didn't want to say anything before when you told me about your mom, because...well, I mean, this sounds kinda bad to say. But I don't remember my mom. So, for most of growing up, she was more of an idea than someone I actually knew enough to miss. It doesn't compare to what you went through."

"It sure as hell does," Caden urged. "I don't care whether you're three or fourteen—a kid needs her mom. At the age you were, you probably needed yours more than I needed mine."

Makenna nuzzled back into Caden's chest, loving the

protectiveness she heard in his voice. "I don't know. Maybe. But that's the thing. I don't know how he did it, but my dad was so great, he managed to fill his shoes and hers. Patrick is seven years older than me. He did a lot to help with me and Collin too. And my dad's sister moved to Philadelphia some time after my mom died. Aunt Maggie was always there when I had a problem I couldn't go to any of the guys with. So, while it's sad to think about not having had a mother, I had a good childhood. I was happy."

"Good," Caden whispered, "that's good."

Caden couldn't believe she'd lost her mother too. It explained a lot about her—she clearly understood loss, even if her experience was different than his. But he had no doubt hers had taught her the empathy and compassion she showed when he'd told his story. He thought maybe he finally understood what people meant when they talked about kindred spirits.

Makenna's back arched when she stretched and yawned, and Caden stifled a groan when her bottom pressed back into his groin. The friction was fantastic but too short. His imagination took off at a sprint. All he could think about was grinding himself into her tight ass and feeling the sensual curves of her hips in his hands as he held her to him.

He was surprised out of his fantasizing when she didn't lean against his chest again, but instead shifted around to face him. He could tell she was sitting on her legs because he felt her knees press against the inside of his thighs. The contact made his groin tighten. He clenched and released his fists, trying so damn badly to let her take the lead. He didn't want to push her past where she wanted to go. But her initiative was fucking sexy. When her hands landed on his chest, his cock twitched and fully hardened. He shifted his hips to make himself more comfortable. She leaned into him. He moaned his appreciation when her breasts fell against his chest as her lips found his chin.

"Hi," she whispered.

"Hi." He wrapped his arms around her body and hugged her to him.

Then her lips found his. Caden groaned as she focused first on the double piercing on the side of his bottom lip. He was relieved she seemed to like his spider bites, as they were called, though he suspected, for *this* woman, he'd rip them the fuck out if she didn't.

Her kiss was soft and slow, exploring, and he savored every pull of her lips, swipe of her tongue, and shifting press of her body. He ran his hands up and down her back enjoying the way the silk of her blouse skimmed against her body. When small moans and whimpers accompanied her kisses, Caden's erection twitched. He shifted his hips. He wanted more of her. He wanted to claim her, make her his.

But he also wanted to see her as he took her. He wanted to learn everything about her body. He wanted to watch her reactions as he used his mouth and hands to please her. And he definitely wanted her to have more than a quick fuck on a floor. She deserved better than that. Much better. And he thought maybe he wanted to give her everything.

Caden had to admit it. He was falling for Makenna. Before tonight, he would've put money against the idea of being able to fall for someone after only knowing them for one day. Good thing he'd never placed that bet.

Makenna's hands cupped his jaws. She leaned into him further, her breasts crushing against his chest. Caden threaded his left hand into the thickness of her hair and took control of the kiss, tilting her head back so he could get better access to her mouth. She tasted phenomenal and, combined with her sweat-heightened scent, was driving him crazy. He shifted his hips again, though she was frustratingly too far away to provide the friction he sought. She sucked hard on his tongue as she drew her head back. He growled and tugged a fistful of her hair. She gave in to his unspoken demand and tilted her head, then Caden laved his tongue against her throat, paying special attention to the spot just below her ear that made her squirm every time.

"I want to touch you, Makenna. Can I?"

She swallowed hard under his lips. "Yes."

"All you have to say is stop."

"Okay," she whispered as she cupped the back of his head with one of her small hands.

His left hand still tangled in her hair, Caden slid his right around her body and cupped the underside of her breast. He paused there, letting her get used to the sensation, giving her time to halt his movements if she wanted. He moaned his approval into the soft skin of her neck when she pressed herself into his touch.

He squeezed her gently and brushed his thumb back and forth. When he stroked her nipple, Makenna rose up onto her knees and reclaimed his mouth. He ravenously swallowed her appreciative moan and set about to elicit others by repeating the movement until she was whimpering.

The darkness intensified every sensation. The sounds of their pleasure were amplified. Textures sprang out against his fingertips. He was swimming in her scent. He couldn't wait to see her, but as he sat holding this sensual woman in his arms, he wasn't complaining he couldn't.

He slid his left hand out of her hair and raked it down her body to her other breast. She rested her forehead on his. He groaned at the feeling of her warm, firm breasts filling his hands as her hair cascaded around both of their faces.

In between panting breaths, she pressed kisses against his forehead as he fondled and stroked and teased her breasts.

She worked her lips and tongue down his temple and he braced himself for her reaction to what she'd find at the edge of his eyebrow. Finally, he felt her tongue, right there. She gasped. "Oh God, more?" she whispered.

Caden had no idea whether her reaction was positive or negative until he heard her moan as she lightly sucked the barbell piercing into her mouth.

He grunted his pleasure at her enthusiastic acceptance and thanked her by concentrating his fingers over her nipples. She cried out, her breath fanning into his ear. He couldn't help thrusting his hips again. He was hard and aching and didn't think he'd ever been as turned on before from kissing.

"Under," Makenna pleaded.

It took a moment for his brain to defog and realize what she was asking. *Hell, yes.*

Together they fumbled at the little pearl buttons on her blouse. Caden slid his fingers inside the satin of her bra cup and found warm erect feminine skin. The proof of her arousal felt incredible, but all his mind could think about was how good he knew she would taste.

⸙⸙⸙

Makenna thought she should be worried about how far this was going, and how much further it might go. But then Caden tugged at her hair or sucked on that sensitive spot under her ear or asked her permission to go just a step further, and she lost all capacity for restraint.

Time and again, Caden's mouth and fingers played her just the right way, as if they'd pleased her many times before. She already thought him an attentive lover, as he repeated every action that elicited a moan or a whimper or writhing from her.

She was hot and wet and needed his big hands on her body. She wouldn't let this go too far, but she had to have something, she had to have more. And she couldn't recall the last time she'd felt so sexy, so passionate. So alive.

The pads of his fingers were rough and felt phenomenal as they gently rubbed and tugged at her sensitive nipples. She could tell her bra was restraining his movements, so she freed her hands from wandering over his body and reached down to tug the satiny cups out of his way.

"You feel so good, Makenna," Caden murmured around their kisses.

She moaned as she felt him stroke his thumbs through the exaggerated cleavage created by the way her disheveled bra pushed her up and in. Needing to feel him too, Makenna's hands dropped to his stomach. She pulled at the softness of his cotton T-shirt until she could slip her hands underneath.

Caden groaned and squirmed when her fingers landed in the trail of small curls leading underneath his waistband. She played with them as she slowly walked her fingers upwards, then finally splayed her fingers out until her hands were flat on him. His stomach twitched and flinched under the teasing touches of her hands. Makenna rubbed her thighs together. She soon found his nipples and lightly scratched her short fingernails over them.

"Aw, hell, Red," he groaned.

"Like that?" She punctuated her question by fingering one of his nipples again while lightly tugging the other. When he grunted his answer, she smiled wickedly against his lips.

She was surprised and disappointed when his hands left her breasts. But then he slid them under her arms and lifted her up higher onto her knees.

"Oh, God, Caden," she cried out when he kissed a circle around her right breast, then rubbed his nose back and forth over her nipple. Her anticipation was nearly at its breaking point for the feel of his mouth there.

He didn't make her wait long. One of his arms embraced her, locking her to his mouth, while his other hand teased the unattended breast. He pulled her so tightly against him she finally had to free one of her hands from underneath his shirt to brace against the wall behind them.

His mouth on her was a riot of sensation. His tongue flicked her nipples. His teeth gently nipped. His lips sucked and tickled and taunted. His piercing bit thrillingly into her skin. Back and forth he went between her breasts until she thought she'd lose her ever-loving mind.

Makenna clenched her thighs together rhythmically, so far gone from his stimulation to her breasts she didn't care if he felt her shifting herself against him.

"Tastes so good, Makenna. Feels so good."

"God, you're killing me."

He plunged his tongue into her cleavage and slowly licked up her chest. It was erotic and thrilling and wanton.

She groaned imagining him plunge that skillful tongue elsewhere.

His fingers returned to her nipples and pinched and twisted as he tilted his head back. Makenna braced her hands on his broad shoulders and looked down, sensing him all around her even though she couldn't see him. She lowered herself slowly until their mouths rediscovered one another in the darkness.

Caden pulled back a little and rubbed his rough cheek against hers. "I want to make you feel good."

"I feel so good with you."

"Mmm...can I make you feel even better?"

Makenna's head grew dizzy from the promise of what he was offering. She couldn't believe she was even considering it, but her body screamed at her for thinking she might turn him down. She nodded her face against his.

"Tell me, Red, you gotta say it out loud. I can't see your face or your eyes, and I don't want to make any mistakes here."

If she'd been just a little unsure a moment ago, she wasn't any longer. "Yes. Please...make me come."

"Oh, fuck, you can't say shit like that right now."

His words brought a smile to her face. She hoped she was affecting him as much as he was her. His words also made her feel bolder, so she teased him, just a little.

"I need to come, so bad. Please?" She bit her bottom lip at her brazenness.

Caden growled, "Mmm, yes." His hands flashed to her hips. He tried to pull her up onto his lap, but her skirt was too tight. Her thighs couldn't spread wide enough to straddle him. "Can I—"

He hadn't needed to ask. Makenna's hands were already at the sides of her thighs hitching her skirt up so she could put her legs over his. She was shaky with want and anticipation. He helped guide her. They both moaned in needy satisfaction when the heated junction of her thighs settled over the bulge in his jeans.

Caden eased her into it. She adored him for it. He started back at her mouth again, exploring her with his tongue while his thumbs and forefingers teased her nipples. She couldn't resist licking and sucking at the metal on his lip, never imagining how incredibly sexy she'd find such piercings. And she especially loved how her attention to them made him grunt in satisfaction.

Now that Makenna had a source of friction, she had to use it. She ground herself against his considerable hardness and whimpered at how good he felt, there. His hands fell to her behind and rocked her against him even harder. With a firm grip on her ass, Caden helped her find a rhythm, encouraging her to use him for her pleasure.

Makenna moaned every time he pulled her against him, though that was nothing compared to what she felt when he finally lowered his left hand to the outside of her panties. His fingers there unhinged her. She cried out and swallowed hard and fought for a breath to ease the dizziness the pleasure caused.

He cupped her mound and grunted. "God, you're so wet."

"Your fault," she gasped.

His voice dripped with arrogance. "Happy to be blamed for this."

"Still smack you," she managed as his fingers began to move, to rub, over the soaked-through satin.

"Maybe later," he rasped. "God, you feel fantastic."

Moaning appreciatively, Makenna clutched herself to Caden's broad shoulders as he helped her thrust against him with one hand while he stroked her with the other.

"Oh, God." Everything—tension, butterflies, tingles, quivers—it all pooled in her lower abdomen.

"I wish I could see you come for me, Makenna."

"Oh!" was all she could manage to gasp out. He moved his fingers harder now, in a circle right over the nerves at the top of her sex. And it was just right. Exactly what she needed to get there.

"Yeah. It's okay, baby. Let go."

"Caden." She let out a high-pitched whimper as pressure built up under his tormenting hand. Her mouth dropped open. He sped up his movements just a little. Pressed just a bit harder.

Her orgasm was going to be tremendous. The whole middle of her body was already tense from the build up of tingling pressure that felt impossibly hard to contain. His fingers were so good. She concentrated hard on the way he was stroking her, on the connection between him and the center of her arousal, and gave herself over entirely to the pursuit of pleasure.

God, just a little more...almost...oh, God.

The elevator whirred and shook. The lights blinked back on.

CHAPTER SIX

Makenna groaned.

The light might as well have been a bucket of ice water—it was uncomfortable and dampened the fire that had raged in her body only seconds before.

She clenched her eyes shut against the unexpected brightness and buried her face in Caden's neck. The light seemed to affect him too. His now-still fingers remained wedged between their bodies, but his face was curled into her to block out the blinding onslaught of the lights.

Several moments passed. The lights remained on. Makenna guessed they were on to stay. Still tucked into Caden, she experimented with opening her eyes enough to get used to the brightness again. It was surprisingly hard. Her eyes protested, blinking and watering for what seemed like minutes.

Finally, she was able to open her eyes all the way. Her shoulders relaxed against Caden's broad chest. And then she realized.

Holy shit! I'm half naked. With a complete stranger. Who currently has his hand up my skirt!

A stranger I've never seen.

Who's never seen me!

What if he thinks I'm a troll? A plain *troll. Or homely—God, I've always hated that word. Homely. Homely. What kind of word is that to describe a person anyway? Oh God, I'm insane.*

The near miss of her orgasm didn't help either. Her body felt strung tight and like fluttery Jell-O all at the same time.

"I guess the power's back to stay this time," Caden said in her ear with a husky, strained voice.

"Um, yeah." Makenna rolled her eyes at her conversational brilliance, certain she was in the process of losing whatever mystique she'd had with the lights out.

Still resting her head on his shoulder, Makenna looked down between them and gaped. Caden's shirt was pushed up around his ribs and all down the left side of his toned stomach lay a swirling abstract tattoo that wrapped around to his back. It was stunning against his skin, which wasn't nearly as fair as her own. Before she really thought about it, her finger traced a curve of the black design. His stomach clenched, and he sucked in a breath at the touch. She smiled.

All at once, she *had* to see the rest of him.

Slowly, she lifted her head and sat back on his lap, keeping her eyes on his stomach all the while. She worried about what he might look like, then hated herself for even thinking about something so shallow. She finally resolved to set those worries aside. Makenna admired so much of what she knew of Caden already, there was no way she wouldn't perceive his internal beauty in his physical appearance, whatever it was.

She fought the instinctive desire to cover herself, to pull the two sides of the gaping silk closed, but she didn't want to hurt his feelings. She didn't want to close herself off to him after all they'd shared.

Her skin tingled all over, as if she could feel the path his eyes blazed as they moved across her body. Finally, she took a deep breath and trailed her eyes up from his stomach, over his tight-fitting, threadbare black T-shirt, across the hard angles of the strong jaw she'd nibbled, to his face.

She couldn't stop trembling, her body unexpectedly flooded with adrenaline as she drank Caden in through her final sense.

He was...*Oh, my God!*...so damn rugged and...masculine...and just...darkly beautiful.

The enticing angle of his jaw combined with full lips and high cheekbones and a strong brow framing intense brown eyes with impossibly long, full eyelashes. His shaved dark brown hair came to a widow's peak in the center of his forehead. Two small silver loops embraced the left side of his bottom lip. The piercing on his right eyebrow was black metal and shaped like a barbell.

He had a face that, with a certain set of his jaw and eyes, could easily appear harsh, intimidating. But she knew he was neither.

With a shaky breath and a hard swallow, Makenna got up the nerve to meet his eyes. He was watching her look him over, his eyes guarded. Not cold, but not warm either. Despite the intimate way they were still touching, Caden's shoulders bunched with tension, and the muscle in his jaw ticked. She got the distinct impression he was bracing himself for rejection.

She'd just been sitting there gawking without saying a word. Hating the idea he might interpret her silence the wrong way, she blurted out, "You're freaking gorgeous!" Her eyes bugged at her unfiltered honesty. She slapped a hand over her mouth and shook her head in embarrassment. She wished the lights would go off again as the blush roared over her skin.

He smiled. And it changed his whole face.

His eyes came to life, sparkling with amusement and happiness. Deep dimples creased his cheeks, bringing out a boyishness not otherwise apparent in his strong masculine features. He quirked an eyebrow at her as his smile shifted to a smirk so playful and sexy it curled her toes against the outside of his thighs.

She dropped her hands from covering her mouth and rested them against the firmness of his stomach. His playfulness brought out hers and, when she felt his hand twitch where it was wedged under her, she groaned and flew at him.

Caden's emotions were so all over the map he couldn't even catalog them. Panic had unleashed a torrent of adrenaline through his system when the lights flashed on. It was soon clear they were on to stay and, as the panic subsided—thanks once again to the calming balm of Makenna's soothing touch and grounding scent, frustration at the god-awful timing of the power's return made Caden grind his teeth as he attempted to acclimate his eyes to the brightness.

The position of his head in the soft curve of her neck allowed him to drink in Makenna's sexy nakedness. And she was...all peaches and cream skin and pert rosy nipples and feminine curves. A milky way of muted freckles ran across the top of her right breast and Caden swallowed against his desire to taste that decorated patch of skin with a long lave of his tongue. The creamy paleness of her thighs highlighted the tan on his dragoned arm where it was still wedged between them, his hand disappearing under the hem of her pulled-up skirt. Even from outside the silky fabric of her panties, Caden could feel the warm wetness of her arousal. His hand absolutely throbbed to resume its movements. He hoped like hell she'd give him the chance.

Caden was so lost in his pleasure at seeing her body he didn't at first realize she was pulling away until his headrest disappeared. He sucked in a breath and girded himself. His mind raced with worry over what she'd think of him. Makenna was a professional, educated, highly intelligent woman. Where she was well adjusted, he was anxious and withdrawn. She looked classy in her gray suit with its little white pinstripes, while he didn't even own a suit and rarely wore anything but jeans except when he worked. Her skin was pure and unblemished, while his was inked, pierced, scarred. Caden wore his past on his body; in fact, he'd used the pain of the tattoo and piercing guns to work through his survivor's guilt. He cringed and clenched his jaw as he wondered what her cop brother would think if they ever met.

Caden cut his eyes from her abdomen to her face as she sat back. Unconsciously, he raised his knees to give her better support as she still straddled him. He watched her face and eyes carefully, looking for any clue, but he couldn't decipher her expression.

And Makenna...Makenna was so very pretty. The hair he already loved was a rich medium red that fell in a mass of loose curls over her shoulders. The way it was parted created a wavy cascade across her forehead and over the edge of her right eye. Her cheeks still bore a flush from their earlier activity, but her skin was otherwise pale and smooth like porcelain, which made her pouty pink lips stand out in contrast. He didn't think she had on any makeup, nor did she need it.

The longer she looked him over without saying anything, the more Caden tensed. His neck and shoulders stiffened as he forced his muscles to stay still under her intense gaze. He could imagine her mentally compiling all of his oddities: "Huge tribal tattoo covering half his abdomen, big dragon down the arm still trapped between my thighs, multiple facial piercings, big ugly scar on the side of his shaved head..." And that wasn't even all of it. *Great*, he could almost hear her thinking, *what the hell have I been kissing in here?*

He trapped the side of his tongue between his molars and bit down, using the pain to distract himself from his worries. If she didn't say something soon...

His jaw dropped open when her eyes finally settled on his. For being pale blue, they weren't the slightest bit cool, but instead exuded the same warmth he already associated with her personality. The weight of her gaze pinned him, as if time was halting and he was balancing precariously on the edge of a cliff, waiting to see whether he'd fall off or be caught by her acceptance.

When her words finally came, Caden couldn't interpret them at first, so different were they from the awkward polite rejection he was expecting.

Gorgeous. Freaking *gorgeous. Hardly. But, Christ, I'll fucking take it.*

Her embarrassment at her outburst released all Caden's tension. He smiled at her until she threw herself at him and literally kissed the silly grin right off his face.

He caught her in an embrace and wrapped his strong arms around her slender shoulders and held her against him. Their kisses went from urgent and needy to deep and languid. She pulled away to breathe, but he couldn't resist pressing his lips to hers for a few more chaste kisses.

She sat back from him and looked down. She fidgeted with her hands, which finally worked their way to the scalloped hem of her pink silk blouse and pulled the edges together across her chest.

Caden cocked his head to one side to figure out what her movements meant. He frowned when she crossed her arms as if to hug herself and worried at her bottom lip with her teeth. "Hey, Mak—"

Out of nowhere, the elevator began moving downward. Makenna gasped. A flashing light caught Caden's eye. The round L was blinking on the bank of call buttons. He figured the elevator was resetting itself by returning to the ground floor, which a more modern elevator would've done when the power first went out.

He squeezed Makenna's biceps. "I'm guessing we're gonna have some company when these doors open," he said, glancing down at her disheveled clothing.

"Oh, yeah, right," Makenna mumbled. She braced herself on his shoulders as she stood. He helped her up. Their movements together turned awkward and clumsy and…just felt all wrong. He frowned and rubbed his hand over his scar when she moved back to "her side" of the elevator and faced the far wall to put herself back together.

When the elevator came to a hard stop, Makenna glanced nervously at the doors as she smoothed over her hair with her hands, then leaned down to pick up her suit jacket.

Thump. Thump.

Makenna squeaked at the unexpected pounding, her hands flying to her chest. She stumbled a little where she'd been trying to step into one of her heels.

Suspecting, Caden started to say, "It's likely just—"

"Arlington County EMS" came a muffled voice. "Anybody in there?"

Caden answered with two pounds of his fist against the still-sealed crease between the doors. "There are two of us," he said as he leaned towards the door.

"Just stay calm, sir. We'll have you out of there in a minute."

"Roger that."

Caden looked to Makenna, worried about the noticeable silence that had come between them in the past minutes.

She stretched a hand forward hesitantly. "Um, sorry, you're..." She pointed at his feet.

Caden glanced down and saw he was standing on the strap of one of her bags. "Oh, shit, I'm sorry." He stepped back and leaned down to retrieve it for her at the same time she did.

They knocked heads. "Ow," they both groaned.

As they reeled back from each other, the doors inched apart. An audience of curious onlookers peered in as Makenna and Caden stood there holding their heads and looking awkward and relieved and embarrassed all at the same time.

❧◦❧◦❧

Makenna felt like a complete idiot, not just for bumping into Caden, but also because the burning tightness behind her eyes told her tears were about to well up.

She thought she knew what his bright smile and sexy smirk and those yummy kisses had meant. But then he gave her those chaste little pecks that tasted like good-bye and didn't say anything. She'd told him he was gorgeous—

freaking gorgeous, thank you very much, and he was...is, so, yeah, there's that—and he hadn't said...anything.

She just knew he'd be disappointed in her appearance. Caden was interesting and edgy and a little dark, and oozed a wounded sexiness that made you want to make his world all better. Makenna could only imagine how conservative, how boring, how *plain* she must look to him. For God's sake, she wasn't even wearing any makeup today. Well, she had been wearing lip gloss, but that had obviously come off a while ago...

She took a deep breath as she slipped her toe-pinching heels on. The doors finally eased open. The rush of cooler air felt fantastic against her overheated skin.

"M.J., are you okay?" Raymond asked, his kind, aging face full of concern.

She slung her bags over her shoulder as she mustered a smile for the building's evening lobby receptionist/guard. "Yep. Still in one piece, Raymond. Thank you."

"Well, that's good, good. Come on out of there already." He reached a wrinkled brown hand out as if she might need his assistance to walk.

Three firemen stood behind Raymond. Their laughter startled Makenna. She frowned at them, wondering what the hell they could possibly find funny about two people being trapped in an elevator for hours on end.

"Grayson!" One of them cackled behind his hand. "Don't worry, man, we're here to save you." The other firemen guffawed.

Makenna glanced over her shoulder in time to see the scowl on Caden's face.

"Laugh it up, Kowalski. You're a goddamned comedian." Caden clasped hands with the guy teasing him. They nudged shoulders in that guy-greeting kind of way.

Raymond led Makenna away from Caden and his fireman friends and chattered on and on about an electrical transformer failing and something about a secondary underground cable and...Makenna didn't really know what he was talking about because she was trying to listen to Caden's conversation.

One of the firemen broke away from giving Caden a hard time and walked over to her. "Are you all right, ma'am? Do you need anything?"

Makenna worked at a faint smile. "No, I'm fine. Just hot and tired. Thank you."

"Have you had anything to drink since you were in there?"

His question made Makenna's throat tighten. She *was* thirsty, now that he mentioned it. She nodded. "I had a bottle of water."

"Okay. That's good." He turned to Raymond. "All right, Mr. Jackson. We're all clear, then." The two men shook hands. "The fire marshal will be by in the morning about these elevators."

"Yes, sir, I understand. I already let 'em know."

The fireman walked around Makenna and returned to the animated conversation between his buddies and Caden.

"Raymond, will you watch my things? I need to use the restroom."

"Of course, M.J. You go right on ahead."

Makenna walked across the lobby, the click of her heels against the marble floor sounded intrusively loud. A tingling sensation at the back of her neck made her swear Caden was watching her, but there was no way she was going to glance behind her to check.

She stepped into the bathroom, and the door closed slowly behind her. The mirror drew her eyes immediately. She groaned at how tired and rumpled she looked. Her hair curled in every direction, wrinkles creased her skirt, and her collar lay askew from how she'd just thrown on her jacket. She shook her head and veered into a stall, wondering if Caden would still be out there when she was done or if he'd leave with the firemen he clearly knew. She wasn't sure what she'd dread more: him waiting for her and the awkwardness between them remaining, or him being gone.

Her stomach fluttered and clenched in nervousness and hunger.

Makenna washed and dried her hands and then gathered up the back of her hair in a handheld ponytail. Leaning forward over the sink, she turned the cold water on and drank long relieving gulps right from the faucet.

Her bathroom visit made her feel a little better. She took a deep breath as she yanked the door open and walked back out into the lobby.

His friends gone, Caden was leaning against the reception desk talking to Raymond.

She blew out a deep breath. A wave of utter relief rushed through her body. He hadn't left. He'd waited.

Then again, what else would a Good Samaritan do?

He smiled as she walked up to them, though this smile was nothing like the face-transforming one he'd given her after she'd blurted her opinion of him. This smile was tight and uncertain. She worried over what it meant.

Ugghhh, she groaned silently. *This is so ridiculous! How did we go from the best conversation of my life to...this?* Makenna decided her fears must be well founded—he must be worrying about how to let her down after...everything. Her deep sense of disappointment was probably out of proportion, but she couldn't help feeling it. She sagged under the weight of it.

Caden scrambled to collect her bags for her. She thanked him as she took them one at a time and hoisted them over her shoulder. They said subdued good nights to Raymond and soon found themselves standing out on a wide sidewalk in the little urban enclave of Rosslyn, just across the river from the heart of D.C. The night air was cool, refreshing. At the end of the block, a line of four Dominion Power trucks idled, their yellow lights circling and flashing.

"Um..." she began, as he said, "Well..."

They both chuckled.

Caden cleared his throat. "Where are you parked?"

"Oh, I take the metro. It's just two blocks that way." Makenna gestured behind her.

Caden frowned. "Is that such a good idea?"

"Oh, yeah. I'll be fine."

"No, really, Makenna. I don't like the idea of you walking to the metro and waiting in the station alone at this time of night."

Makenna shrugged, feeling warmed just a little by his concern.

"Let me take you home. My Jeep's just down the street here."

"Oh, well, I don't want to—"

He reached forward and grasped her hand. His touch provided almost as much relief as the water had earlier. "I'm not taking no for an answer. It's not safe for you to be walking around at this hour by yourself. Come on." He tugged at her gently, still allowing her to make up her mind.

"Oh…okay. Thanks, Caden. It's not too far."

"I know." He threaded his big fingers between her smaller ones. "Not that it would matter if it was."

She looked up at his profile and smiled. He was a lot taller than she was, and she liked tall men. He glanced down at her and squeezed her hand.

Caden led her around the corner of her building to a side street. He paused at a shiny black Jeep with no top and opened her door for her.

"Thanks." She reached inside and set her bags down on the floor of the passenger seat on top of a baseball glove. Her skirt made it a little difficult to get up and in. She blushed as she hiked it up a bit.

Caden shut her door and a moment later filled the driver's seat next to her. The Jeep rumbled to life. Makenna braced herself against the door as Caden pulled a U-turn out of the parking space. The breeze picked up tendrils of her hair and made them dance across her face. She quickly gathered the length of it in her hand to keep it from blowing too much.

"Sorry," Caden muttered as he turned onto the street fronting her building. "I go without the top whenever I can," he said in a low voice. "More open." He shrugged his shoulders.

As realization of what he was saying hit her, Makenna opened her mouth. But she couldn't find the words to tell him how brave she thought he was. So she just said, "It's okay. The air feels great."

Soon they were flying up Wilson Boulevard, the string of green lights and mostly empty streets making the trip quicker than usual. Sitting on his right side, Makenna had her first opportunity to really see the full extent of the long crescent-shaped scar that began over Caden's ear and jagged back to the edge of his hairline on his neck. In the flashing streetlights, she could tell the scar tissue didn't grow hair, making the curve of it stand out against the surrounding dark brown.

Caden must've sensed her gaze, because he glanced over at her and quirked a lopsided smile that made her stomach clench in want and disappointment that their evening was moments from ending.

A few quick turns later, the Jeep pulled into the circular drive of her condo complex. Makenna pointed out the entrance to the residences, and Caden eased into a space adjacent to the lobby door.

The usually calming sound of the central fountain bubbling was just discernible over the Jeep's idling. Makenna took a tired breath as the weight of the day pressed her back into the comfortable leather seat.

It was time to say good-bye.

CHAPTER SEVEN

Caden hadn't stopped cursing at himself since she'd disappeared into the bathroom. Somehow, he'd fucked things up with Makenna. Now she was acting distant and uncertain and even a little shy around him. And even though he hadn't known her very long, all of these seemed out of character for the Makenna he'd come to know and…really like. *His* Makenna was warm and open and confident. He had the distinct feeling he'd done something to clip her wings. And he was pissed as hell at himself, especially because he didn't know what to do to fix it.

And he was running out of time.

At least she'd agreed to let him drive her home. He spent the drive thinking about what to say to her and how to say it. Her stare didn't help his concentration. There was no avoiding the clear view she'd have of the ugliness of his scar. Plastic surgery when he was fifteen had smoothed out the worst of the tissue and mostly restored a natural hairline at the back of his neck, but it was still big and obvious and often made people first meeting him uncomfortable because it was hard to avoid looking at. It didn't help that the curved, thin line of ruined skin couldn't grow hair, which made it stand out even more. He thought of the damn thing as his first tattoo—it certainly stood out as much as any of his colorful ink.

He let her have a good look, though. Because he didn't look normal and never would. And though she seemed to accept everything he'd revealed to her so far, he knew he could be a lot to take on board. He wanted her to be sure. So he only smiled over at her. He took out his tension on the gear shift gripped tightly in his right hand.

There was little he could do to drag out the trip to her condo. Even in mid-day traffic, it was no more than a fifteen-minute ride from Rosslyn to Clarendon. And, of course, when he wouldn't have minded some red lights, every one was green.

The Jeep idling at the curb, Caden shifted in his seat. "Makenna, I—"

"Caden—" she started at the same time.

They both smiled weakly. Caden swallowed a groan. Makenna's hair was windblown around her shoulders and her eyes looked tired, but she was so damn pretty. "You first," he said. *Chicken shit.*

"Thanks for keeping me such good company tonight." She gave him her first genuine smile.

Hope filled his chest. "It was my pleasure, Makenna."

She nodded and reached down to grasp the straps to her bags in one hand while her other went to the door handle. Caden's jaw clenched. "Okay, then, I guess…good night, then." She engaged the handle and pushed the door open.

His stomach rolled. She shifted herself and hopped down onto the sidewalk, then turned to drag her bags behind her. *What the fuck, Caden, stop her. Tell her.* "I'd like to—"

She shoved the door shut, drowning out his words, and leaned against the open window. He swore she looked sad but wasn't sure, just didn't know her facial expressions well enough to read them. Yet. *Please let there be a "yet."*

"It's okay. I understand."

Caden gaped, then pressed his lips into a tight line. *Understand? Understand what?*

She tapped her hand twice against the door interior. "Thanks for the ride. See ya."

"Uh, yeah." He ran his hand roughly over his scar as she turned, slung her bags over her shoulder, and walked across the wide sidewalk towards the brightly lit windowed lobby.

Uh, yeah? UH, YEAH?

When she was almost to the door, Caden threw the Jeep in first and pressed his foot on the accelerator. He pulled out into the drive. The growing distance from Makenna felt so damn wrong that Caden stopped in the middle of the street and looked back over his shoulder.

Makenna was standing in the lobby. Watching him.

He growled. *Fuck. This.*

Caden slammed the transmission into reverse. The tires screeched against the pavement as he jolted the vehicle back into the spot. He pulled forward just as gracelessly to straighten out. He wrenched the keys from the transmission and smacked the headlights off and heaved his body against the door, which he slammed shut.

Stalking around the back of the Jeep, he glared up at Makenna—glaring not so much at her as at his own idiocy for not making things right before the eleventh goddamned hour.

Her eyes widened. Her lips froze somewhere between a smile and an O. She pushed and held the door open for him.

And he hoped for all he was worth he was correctly reading the desire on her face.

He crowded right up into her space, pressed his body against hers—trapping her against the glass of the door behind her, plunged his hands into her hair until he was cupping the nape of her neck, and devoured her lips with his.

He groaned at the goodness of touching her again, like this. It was the first time anything had felt right since he'd held her on his lap in the elevator.

⌀⌀⌀⌀⌀

Anticipation stole Makenna's breath—and then Caden did with his forceful kiss. *Oh my God oh my God oh my God he came back! He came back!*

His demanding tongue tasted so damn good, and his piercing bit deliciously against her lip from the aggressive way he pursued her over and over. His hands tugged and massaged at her hair and neck. He just surrounded her. The difference in their height made Caden lean down over her.

The way he forced her head back commanded her to open up to him. With the metal handle of the door pressing into her back, she felt completely enveloped in him, in his ardor, his scent. The world dropped away. There was just Caden.

Her hand fisted in his black shirt. He stepped closer. They panted. Their bodies heaved against one another. She moaned at the possessiveness of his grip. There was nothing shy or tentative or questioning about the way he was handling her. She felt claimed. She felt euphoric.

A tantalizing sound somewhere between a purr and a growl erupted from low in his throat. His hands continued to grip her, but he leaned his forehead against hers and pulled his lips away. "I'm sorry. I couldn't let you go."

"Don't be sorry for that," she rasped and swallowed. "Never be sorry for that."

"Makenna—"

"Caden, I—"

He clamped his lips over her mouth, their noses smashing. This time his sound was very clearly a growl. "Woman," he said against her lips, "would you let me talk already?"

The longing and frustration in his voice made her smile. She nodded. His lips quirked against hers, and he kissed her again, a series of quick pecks against her mouth.

By the time he finally started to talk, Makenna felt a little dizzy. His breath was sweet against her face. His stubble chafed at her cheek. He bored those deep brown eyes into her, pinning her against him in every possible way.

"I've never…you're just…" He heaved a sigh. "Aw, hell. I like you, Red. I want to be with you. I want you to argue with me some more. I want to lie in your arms again. I want to touch you. I…I just…"

Hope and happiness filled and warmed her chest. He'd come back for her. He wanted her.

Smiling, Makenna reached a hand up behind her neck and grabbed one of his. He hesitated to release her, but finally let her pull his hand around to her mouth, where she pressed a big open-mouthed kiss onto the head of his dragon. She grinned up at him. "Come upstairs," she breathed. "I make a mean omelet. And I'm starving."

Her smile finally returned to brighten his face. He squeezed her hand and kissed her forehead. "Okay. I could definitely eat."

When Caden stepped away to allow her to turn back into the lobby, Makenna immediately missed the hard heat of his body all against hers. She squeaked when he grabbed at her bags, jerking her back a half step.

"Let me," he said as he pulled the straps away and slung them over his shoulder.

My Good Sam.

Out of habit, she stepped to the bank of elevators and pressed the button. This late at night, the door dinged and opened immediately. She turned to assess Caden's reaction before stepping in.

He rolled his eyes and motioned her forward, grumbling under his breath.

She was giddy things were turning out so differently than she'd feared just fifteen minutes before. Her joy bubbled over. She burst out laughing, then grasped his hand and pulled him into their second elevator of the night. "Come on. Lightning doesn't strike twice. Usually."

She hit the button for the fourth floor and stepped against him and nuzzled his chest. He stroked her hair and she melted.

The elevator reached her floor and opened up onto a rectangular space with halls running in opposite directions. She led Caden out and to the left, down to the fifth door on the right. "This is me."

She reached into her open purse still on his shoulder and found her key ring, then turned and opened the door. Smiling over her shoulder at him, she pushed into her apartment and flicked on the hall light, which illuminated her small tidy kitchen as well. She walked to the kitchen counter and dropped her keys, then turned and unburdened Caden of her bags, and plopped those onto the counter, too.

Sliding his hand around her neck, he kissed her again. Gently, adoringly. "Do you mind if I use your bathroom?"

"Of course not." She pointed behind him. "Just down that hall. I'm going to change out of my work clothes."

"Okay." He brushed her cheek with his big fingers. She leaned into the touch. Then he turned away.

Makenna floated across her small apartment to her bedroom. She stumbled into her walk-in closet, kicking off her heels as she went, and stripped off her rumpled and grimy clothes. She breathed a deep sigh of relief when she was finally naked. The idea of a cool shower took root in her mind and sounded so delicious she finally gave in. She piled her hair on top her head to keep it dry and just stood for a moment as the water streamed over her. Finally, she grabbed the bar of Ivory and ran it quickly over her skin. Minutes later, she was back in her closet and feeling a lot more like a human being.

She grabbed a pretty lavender lace bra and panty set, hoping against hope he'd actually see it, then slid into a pair of gray yoga pants and a soft lavender V-neck shirt. In her bathroom, she brushed her teeth and reworked her hair into a ponytail. She stretched her arms up over her head and luxuriated in feeling more comfortable than she'd been in hours.

When she strolled back out into the adjoining living room, she found Caden perusing her display of family photographs. She paused and leaned against the corner of the wall for a moment, just enjoying the look of him wandering around her apartment. He'd taken off his socks and shoes and now padded around barefoot, the frayed hem of his blue jeans just dragging on the floor. She was truly pleased he'd made himself at home in her space.

"Liking what you see?"

The blush roared up her cheeks. She chuckled and debated how to answer. It was late, she was tired, and she *was* interested. So she threw caution to the wind—he had come back for her, after all. "Yes, very much."

He looked over his shoulder and offered a lopsided grin that beckoned her to come stand next to him. She glanced up at the collection of photos he'd been admiring. "Those are my brothers." She pointed each of them out as she said their names. "That one's Patrick. Ian. And that's Collin. And me, of course."

"You're not the only Red in your family, I see."

Makenna laughed. "Uh, definitely not. Though, Patrick and Ian's hair looks more brownish than mine. Collin, though, had to deal with 'Carrot Top' comments all through school." She pointed to another frame. "The red was my mom's fault, as you can see." She watched Caden as he studied the picture of her mother holding Makenna on her lap just a few months before she'd died. It was her favorite because the family resemblance was so obvious. Her father told her all the time she looked just like her mother.

Lost in the image for a moment, she was surprised when Caden's hand tugged on her ponytail. She was even more surprised when her hair spilled down around her shoulders.

"Sorry," he murmured as he ran his fingers through her freed locks. "I spent all night imagining touching your hair."

Her blush returned, softer this time. His directness was one of her favorite things about him. She wasn't sure what to say in response, though, so she closed her eyes and just enjoyed the feeling of his strong fingers. After a few moments, she opened her eyes and found him staring intently at her. She smiled. "That feels nice. You're going to put me to sleep, though."

His smile made his eyes crinkle and shine. "That wouldn't be so bad, if you fell asleep with me again."

Makenna pressed her hands against her cheeks when she felt them heat again. Her pale skin tone showed everything. She grabbed his hand and pressed a kiss into his palm. "Come on, I promised to feed you."

❧❧❧

Caden was ecstatic he'd read her right, that she'd wanted him to come back for her. He'd had to pull back from kissing her down in the lobby, because his imagination already had him buried inside of her against the windows. And he didn't want her to get it in her head he'd only come back for sex.

He wanted sex. That was true. The clingy form-fitting pants and the shirt that emphasized the firmness and roundness of her luscious breasts didn't help those desires. But he also wanted a chance.

Standing there in her apartment, feeling so welcomed and wanted, he was almost ready to believe she would give him one.

Still holding his hand, she walked them into the kitchen. "You can sit at the bar if you like. Want something to drink?"

"I'd love something to drink," he said, "but I don't need to sit. I can help." He watched Makenna move around her kitchen and admired the way her casual outfit highlighted her feminine curves.

She turned and smiled at his offer, then sat a cutting board and sharp knife in front of him. "You can help me chop, then. What do you like in your omelets?" She listed what she had. They settled on ham and cheese. The cold fizzy Coke she gave him relieved his parched throat.

Caden diced the ham while Makenna cracked the eggs into a glass bowl and beat them. He really liked working with her in the kitchen. It felt normal. And normal wasn't something he'd had a whole lot of in his life.

Makenna peeked over at him. They both smiled. He chopped. She stirred. Then he stole a glance at her. They both chuckled.

He was having fun with her, liked their flirting and the now-comfortable quiet between them. But it was hard not to touch her. His fingers itched to tuck her hair behind her ear. Her bottom looked so pat-able in her snug cotton pants. When she blushed, his lips yearned to taste the heat of it on her cheeks. Though, he knew if he touched her, he wouldn't be able to stop. So he busied his hands with his contribution to their meal.

Makenna wiped her hands on a towel and bent over. The sound of metal clanging made it clear she was looking for a pan. But all Caden could focus on was the way her backside pushed out toward him from how she'd bent at the waist. He took another long drink of Coke, but kept his eyes glued on her.

She grumbled and stood up, then placed her hands on her hips. "Oh, there it is," she said. She walked over to the sink and turned the water on. "Crap!" Something pinged against the floor.

Caden chuckled at the little show she didn't even realize she was putting on for him. His humor died in his throat, however, when she bent over again, retrieving the ring she'd apparently taken off and dropped.

He couldn't help it. All his focus on her rear had made him hard again. Their night together had turned out to be one long delicious tease, but now they were safe and cozy and alone in her apartment, so comfortably and intimately preparing a meal together. And he was going crazy wanting her.

Setting the little silver ring back on the counter, Makenna squirted some dish soap into the frying pan and quickly scrubbed it clean. Caden picked the towel up off the counter and walked up tight behind her. He wrapped his arms around her and plucked the pan out of her hands, then dried it quickly and set it aside on the counter. Makenna turned off the water.

Caden braced his hands against the edge of the sink on either side of her body and leaned the full press of him against her. Bending himself around her, he nipped and kissed her neck and jaw. She moaned and pushed her little body back against his.

He hadn't been so forward as to grind his erection into her, but she clearly felt it when she pressed herself back, because she gasped and clutched the edge of the sink in front of her.

Caden couldn't stop. The heat of her body against him, there, made it impossible for him to want anything other than all of her. He had to have her.

He had to have her, now.

CHAPTER EIGHT

The suddenly electric atmosphere in the kitchen rippled across Makenna's skin.

"Makenna," Caden whispered against her neck as he wrapped his arms around her.

She couldn't hold back the whimper that spilled from her open lips. His embrace felt so good, especially when he slid one arm up until it tucked under her breasts and the other down until his hand gripped one of her hips. She loved the way he used the leverage he gained from his firm hold to control the movement of their bodies.

The feel of him hard and needful behind her drove her insane with want. Her body readied itself immediately. She rubbed her thighs together as wetness settled against her panties.

With one hand, Caden cupped her jaw and drew her head to the right. Then he claimed her mouth, sucking on her lips and exploring her with his tongue. She let him lead, loving how commanding he was. He wasn't rough at all, but he took what he wanted. And she was willing to give him everything.

Makenna reached a hand back and grabbed his hip, her fingers extending further around to rest on the clenching muscle of his rear. Then, just to make sure her intentions were clear, she grasped his ass and pulled him against her. She swallowed his groan as their kisses grew more urgent, more desperate.

When he bent his knees and rolled his hips into her ass, she cried out—a sound he elongated by kneading her breast and rubbing her nipple over and over with the heel of his thumb.

Minutes passed as they writhed against each other within the firm embrace of Caden's strong arms. His warm wet kisses were languorous and dizzying. His quick breaths and throaty groans sounded out a language her body understood, responded to, and needed to hear again and again.

Her hands shook with the need to touch him. Finally, she reached her free hand up and wrapped it around the back of his head so she could stroke him encouragingly. He read her movements correctly. His kisses came faster, harder.

When his lips moved to her jaw, then her ear, then her throat, her chest heaved and her body ached with want. "Please," Makenna finally begged.

She tried to turn in his arms but he gripped her tighter, for just a moment. Then he relented, releasing his hold long enough for her to move. She moaned in relief when she could wrap her arms fully around his neck and hold him to her. He kept her trapped against the counter, but she reveled in the tight press because it allowed her to torment his obvious arousal with her thrusting hips and writhing abdomen.

His hands blazed a teasing trail from her breasts to the sides of her stomach to her hips, and back again. She squirmed under his touch and needed more of it. Needed it on her skin.

She withdrew her arms and found the hem of her shirt. He pulled his body off hers just enough to allow them to work together to remove it. She dropped it to the floor, relieved to feel his big hands exploring her skin with such enthusiasm.

Caden's eyes raked over what she'd revealed to him. Makenna blushed at the intensity of his observation. "Aw, Red, you're so very pretty."

Makenna's heart exploded at the affirmation his words provided. Whatever insecurity about her ordinariness she might've still harbored in the back of her mind disappeared completely at his exclamation.

He dropped his head to her chest and licked and nibbled and kissed all along the lacy edge of her bra. As he flicked at her covered nipple with his rigid tongue, his arms reached around behind her. Her bra fell loose into their arms and soon it joined her shirt somewhere on the floor.

Makenna's moan was loud and needy when he cupped her breasts and alternated sucking on one nipple, then the other. Her hands flew to his head. She held him to her as she arched her back to offer him better access. His mouth was driving her insane. She'd never had someone lavish such attention to her breasts, and she'd certainly never felt so weak and wanton from it. She snaked one hand down his back and fisted his black shirt between his shoulder blades. "Off," she demanded as she tugged at it.

He reached back, his lips still greedily devouring a nipple, and wrenched his shirt off, only dropping his mouth from her when he absolutely had to.

"Oh, God," she murmured appreciatively as her eyes surveyed his broad chest.

There was so much more to him than she'd seen in the elevator. The large tribal tattoo that curled around the left side of his abdomen accompanied a beautiful open-faced yellow rose on his upper left pectoral muscle. The dragon roared up his right forearm, then the skin was unmarked until her eyes reached the very top of his bicep, where a red four-pronged badge sat with a tiny fire hydrant, hook, and ladder surrounding a gold number seven. His browned skin revealed the amount of time he must've spent without a shirt under the summer sun, and made the vibrant colors of his tattoos stand out even more.

Her original impression was so right—he was freaking gorgeous. She wanted to explore every inch of him, to trace every ridged muscle and every tattoo with her fingers and tongue.

Makenna's mouth went right to the rose. Her hands clutched the firm muscles of his sides. Caden threaded his fingers into her hair and held her to him. Her tongue ran around the edge of one of the lower yellow petals before trailing down and finding his nipple, which was right at the natural height of her mouth.

"So good," he rasped. He pressed a kiss onto her hair.

She flicked her thumb back and forth over the skin she'd made wet, so she could pay attention to his other nipple as well. He groaned at her teasing touch. She smiled at getting him back for how deliciously he'd tormented her earlier.

His skin felt so good under her fingers, and tasted better—just a little salty from how hot they'd been in the elevator. She imagined them in the shower together, using her own bare, soapy hands to wash the day off him. A smile formed where her lips were still pressed against his chest. *Another time*, she mused. *Please let there be another time.*

All this slow exploration made her ache. The cleft between her legs was wet and throbbing. Her body begged for the relief of his touch. And she hoped and prayed his body was making the very same pleas.

She sucked his right nipple into her mouth and flicked her tongue against it until he fisted his hand in her hair. She couldn't tell if he was holding her in place or trying to pull her away. Maybe both. But she could tell, either way, he liked it, because he grunted and rocked his hips into her.

Experimentally, she dropped her fingers from teasing his nipples and drew lazy circles over his abdomen, enjoying the way his muscles flinched and clenched under her light touch. His breaths quickened when her fingers swirled in the line of brown hair disappearing under his waistband. Without pausing, she continued down over the denim and cupped his considerable length in the palm of her hand.

"Christ," he groaned, then thrust against where she was rubbing him.

His fingers returned to her nipples. She whimpered and tilted her head back to look up at him. His eyes blazed. He leaned forward and pressed his lips against hers, then pushed his tongue into her mouth.

She went from rubbing him to squeezing him through his jeans.

"Makenna," he rasped, his voice soft and seductive, "I want you so much." He pulled back until they could see one another, then reached up and tucked her hair behind her ear. "What do you want?"

Reluctantly, she pulled her hand away from stroking him and brought both hands up to cup his face. "Everything. I want everything with you."

❧❧❧

Blood pounded through Caden's body. His senses were on fire—her incredible scent, the sounds of her needy whimpers and moans, the satiny-soft feel of her skin under his fingers, the salty-sweet taste of her flesh. As he kissed and touched her, he watched her intently, eager to learn what she liked, finding pleasure in what gave her pleasure.

But when she started exploring him, he thought he'd lose his fucking mind. She'd tugged in silent demand for him to remove his shirt, which he'd done more than willingly, then she started devouring the skin of his chest after drinking him in through her eyes. Every movement of her mouth and hands was playful and sensual and set his body to throbbing, to begging for more.

And she'd given it to him. The press of her small, strong hand around his erection was irresistible. He hadn't held back from using the incredible friction he'd so badly needed and she'd so willingly provided.

And then she confirmed she wanted him too, just the way he wanted her. Her words resonated everywhere—a long-sought satisfaction calmed his mind and a comforting heat filled his chest. Those feelings were magnificent, life-giving—and more than he ever expected to experience.

In that moment, though, it was his cock that most reacted to her words, to the fulfillment they promised. And, as if her words weren't enough, she dropped her hands from lovingly holding his face and hooked the fingers of her right hand into his waistband, then turned and led them from the kitchen.

Caden smiled at her methods and followed her eagerly as she guided him past the small dining table, through the living room, and into her most private sanctuary. The room was square and dim, the distant kitchen light and the filtered light of the moon through the sheer curtains providing the only illumination.

She turned to face him, but didn't drop her fingers. Instead, she added her other hand and easily worked the line of buttons open. Looking him in the eye, she shoved at the heavy denim fabric where it hugged his hip and at the same time snaked her other hand inside his snug boxers until she gripped him skin-to-skin.

Caden's mouth fell open at the thrilling sensation of her soft fingers stroking his hard length. He held her gaze, pleaded with his eyes for her to continue on.

"Fuck. What are you doing to me?" She couldn't know it, but his question was about so much more than the wonderful movements of her little hand.

When she tugged at his jeans with her free hand, Caden quickly pushed them and his boxers down over his hips. He followed her gaze as she admired him. Her hand looked so good stroking him. He had to close his eyes against the erotic image so he could conjure up more control—he wanted this to go on for a long time. And she was already pushing him.

She let out a moan that dragged his eyes open again. He wasn't the only one squirming at the picture of her hand around his cock. Makenna's mouth hung open. A flush expanded out across her heaving bare chest. Every few seconds, her tongue darted out across her bottom lip.

Out of nowhere, she gripped his length more firmly and wrapped a hand around his waist, then walked them backward until her legs hit the bed. She sat down and pulled him another step closer until his groin was even with her face.

Caden gaped. Desire had never looked more beautiful than when she tilted her eyes up to him and sucked his head between her pink lips. He gasped as the wet heat wrapped around him.

"Christ, Makenna..."

He clenched and unclenched his hands and was surprised when one of her hands found one of his. She pulled his palm to her head. Drawing back from him for just a moment, she said, "Show me what you like."

Her offer astounded him and he grew in her mouth. Need led him to twist his fingers into her hair. But there wasn't anything she was doing he didn't love the hell out of. "Trust me, baby, you know what you're doing. I can't believe...your mouth is perfection."

She moaned around his length. He shivered at the sensation. The suction of her mouth and the teasing flicks of her tongue melted his insides. He gave into the urge and applied the lightest pressure against the back of her head with his fist. He resisted thrusting into her mouth though, not because his body wasn't screaming for him to do so, but because he wanted to let her lead this, and he didn't want to finish this way. And he was walking a very fine line.

Too fine, in fact.

If he didn't make her stop now, he wouldn't be able to resist the pleasure she was drawing out of him. He tugged at her hair, gently urging her to let go.

She released him and looked up with wet, shiny lips and a self-satisfied smile. He smirked, then leaned down and kissed her.

Still attacking her mouth, Caden dropped to his knees, and his hands fell to her thighs. After a moment, he walked his fingers up to her waistband.

"Lift," he ordered.

After he had peeled the last of her clothing from her, he sat back on his heels and drank in the beauty of her femininity. Very deliberately, he raked his gaze over her, over the plump rounded swells of her rising and falling breasts, over the soft curve of her porcelain stomach, down to the patch of damp red curls at the top of her sex.

Makenna's heart slammed against her breastbone. Each progression of their actions stretched her jangling nerves more taut and further readied her between her thighs. Once she'd had him in her room and in her hand, she knew she had to taste him.

She'd reveled in the warm heavy weight of him in her mouth, in the way his jaw dropped in pleasure, and in the deep groan that filled the room the first time she'd taken him all the way in to the back of her throat. The blaze in his eyes was so intense when she looked up at him it drove her harder. She wanted to bring him the pleasure he'd been bringing her all night. And, when she'd noticed a jagged four-inch scar just above his right hip, she redoubled her efforts, sucking him in deeper and running her tongue over him more vigorously.

This man had been through hell and back at a very young age. Yet, he'd survived without succumbing to the bitterness and resentment and despair that must've sometimes lured him. Instead, he was the kind of man who helped other people—for a living and as a matter of course. And he was relentlessly kind and quietly funny and more goddamned sexy than any man had a right to be.

So she'd wanted to do that for him. She'd wanted to concentrate all her efforts on bringing him pleasure. Again and again she'd hollowed out her cheeks and sucked hard as she brought her mouth up his entire length. Just as she reached his head, she'd abruptly stop sucking and plunge her mouth down around him again, taking him into the back of her throat. His ragged breathing and muttered curses were thrilling.

She almost whined when his gentle tugging pleaded with her to release him. But she was so eager to see where they'd go next she didn't think on it long.

Soon, she was watching Caden rake his eyes across her naked body. They were barely touching, but the moment felt so erotic. It was more than just sexual, though— Makenna was almost certain that within the mask of desire he wore was another emotion—adoration. And it made her feel so safe and secure to be with him this way.

God, he looked so freaking sexy kneeling between her legs. Caden Grayson was a big man, in every sense of the term. To see him before her like that...

And then he crawled closer. She had the distinct impression of a predator stalking his prey.

"Lie back," he encouraged as his hands walked up to her hips and his body settled between her thighs. She complied and reclined onto her elbows so she could watch him.

Then, with no pretense at all, his head dropped to the cleft of her legs. He laved a long hard stroke of his tongue through her wet folds, boring his eyes into hers all the while.

"Oh, Caden!" She felt his tongue all the way down to her curling toes.

"You taste as good as I knew you would," he murmured right against her. He lowered his face to her red curls and kissed her softly, then he further separated her thighs with his shoulders and licked her most sensitive skin over and over again.

Makenna's hands fisted against the soft green comforter under her. Weakened by the pleasure he so expertly provided, she dropped all her weight back against the bed and luxuriated in the play of his tongue against her. She uttered a near-constant string of encouragements and pleadings, but couldn't find it in herself to be the least bit self-conscious.

She'd had guys go down on her before, but no man had ever seemed as responsive to her body's cues as Caden. The way he paid attention to her soon had him treating her to an alternating rhythm of long hard strokes from her opening to her clit and intense bursts of flicks and sucks concentrated on the latter. Every once in a while the metal rings on his lip dragged across her labia. She found the unexpected sensation surprisingly decadent.

He was playing her body, commanding her pleasure, eliciting the same notes from her again and again. When he added his thumb to his efforts, stroking repeatedly over her clit while his tongue circled and dipped into her opening, every nerve ending concentrated itself at the center of her body.

"Caden, oh, my God. Oh, my God." Pure white-hot energy was flowing through her, rising in her, threatening to break her apart.

He responded to her words by rubbing her harder, faster, drinking from her more deeply.

"I'm...oh, I'm...."

She lost her words to a loud moan as a glorious explosion of sensation began under Caden's talented mouth and ricocheted through every cell in her body. Muscles flexed and contracted throughout her in a wave. She groaned as he refused to let up one bit, continuing to stimulate her over-sensitive skin in a way that extended her orgasm endlessly.

"Holy shit," she squeaked out between shuddering breaths.

When Caden pressed a line of kisses from her right thigh over her right hip, she felt the smile curling his lips. Then he playfully bit her hipbone. She screamed out a throaty laugh.

She liked someone who didn't have to be serious during sex, who could smile and laugh. It was just one more thing they had in common.

But she wasn't done with him yet.

Saving them the awkward conversation, Makenna flopped her right arm out on the bed and pointed to her night stand. "Drawer. Condom. On you. Now."

"Mmm. Yes, ma'am." He pushed himself into a standing position and kicked off his jeans which still hung around his knees.

Makenna licked her lips as he strode the three steps around her bed and reached into the drawer. His body was all taut lean muscle and moved with a quiet power. There wasn't enough light to make out the details of the designs, but she could see more ink decorated his shoulder blades.

Later, she planned to explore every inch of his amazing body. But just then, she needed him with her, in her. She needed a resolution to the hours of build-up between them.

Caden tossed the silver wrapper aside and unrolled the condom over his thick length. Makenna blushed though she couldn't look away—she'd always found that action particularly erotic. When he looked at her and smiled, she pushed herself back up to the pillows and held out a hand to him.

He crawled over top of her and lowered his weight onto her. She'd always loved that feeling, the weight of a man's body covering hers, and it never felt better than when Caden's tall muscular frame encompassed hers so fully, so lovingly.

Taking her head gently into his hands, he pressed closed-mouth kisses against her lips until she pushed her tongue out and encouraged his lips to part. She could taste herself on him, something else that had always driven her mad because it was like tasting the pleasure he'd given her all over again. When Caden groaned around her probing tongue, she kissed him more deeply and sucked hard on his tongue until he broke free of her and playfully bit at her jaw in punishment for her teasing.

He stroked his fingers over her hair, then rubbed her cheekbone with his knuckles. "Are you sure?"

She smiled and nodded. "I'm very sure. You?"

He chuckled. "Um..." He pursed his lips and looked up at the ceiling, putting on what she assumed was supposed to be a thinking face.

She reached her hand around him and not so lightly smacked his ass.

His eyes dropped back to her. His mouth fell open.

Makenna cocked an eyebrow. "I *told* you I would smack you."

The laugh he let loose sounded so purely happy she grinned even though she was trying to look put out.

"That you did. I like a woman who keeps her word." He kissed her again, softly this time. "Yes, I am very sure I want you, Makenna. Can I have you?" He gazed so intently in her eyes she almost thought he was asking for more than just permission to possess her body.

"Yes," she whispered, intending her answer as the reply to every way he might've meant his question.

~~~~~

Pushing himself up onto one elbow, Caden reached a hand down between them and stroked his fingers over Makenna's soft folds. He wanted to make sure she was ready. She was. Her responsiveness to him was thrilling. He centered his cock over her opening and met her eyes. And then he slowly pushed himself into her.

He groaned at the feeling of being inside of her, at the idea that maybe, just maybe, he'd found a place, a woman, he could belong to for all time.

The tight walls of her most private place gripped him fiercely, surrounding him in white-hot heat and velvet softness. He moaned low in his throat. "You feel so good."

When he filled her completely, he stilled and let them both savor the sensation.

She clutched at his shoulders. "So do you. God, I feel..."

He studied her face when she trailed off and watched a blush bloom on top of the flush their activities had already brought out in her skin. Now he was intrigued—he really wanted her to finish that sentence.

"What? What do you feel?" He strained to resist the instinct to move his hips.

She shook her head and flexed her hips, driving him deeper into her. It felt incredible, but he recognized the diversionary tactic for what it was.

He pulled his cock out until just the tip of his head was still inside her. Tremors shook his shoulders with the effort it took not to sink back into her. "Tell me."

She groaned. "Caden, I need you." He smiled at the pleading in her voice. She wrapped her legs around his hips and pressed her heels into his ass. But he was too strong for her to be able to force him to move. She pouted, but relented. "I *felt* so incredibly full."

His ego buoyed, he didn't hesitate to recreate the feeling for her, and plunged immediately back into her gripping heat. "Like that?"

"Yes, just like that," she moaned. "*God.*"

He remembered his earlier desire to see her when he took her and pushed himself up onto his arms. His hands settled on both sides of her ribs. He grunted appreciatively at the full view the position gave him.

He moved in her then, flexing his hips over and over, driving his rigid length into her slick tightness. Her muscles sucked at him as she shifted positions. He finally hooked his right arm under her left leg to force her more open underneath him. The change allowed him to plunge even deeper.

He shook his head at how good it all felt. "So tight. Christ, so wet."

She clamped her teeth down on her bottom lip and groaned as his repeated thrusts rocked into her. Her blue eyes were hooded with desire and flashed with a wondrous affection for him.

Caden returned her intense gaze. He caught her every movement, her every reaction to their joining. His mind began a catalog of information on Makenna he hoped he'd be fleshing out for a long time to come.

When she reached her wandering hands up to cup her own breasts and stroked her fingers over her nipples, he hummed in approval. "That's right. That looks so good."

He liked that she had the confidence to seek out pleasure during sex. She wasn't reserved. She didn't play games. Instead, she was real and completely guileless in the pursuit of their pleasure. Her honesty made her even sexier to him.

When Makenna's eyes dropped down to where they were joined, his eyes followed.

"Fuck," he murmured as he watched his wet cock slide in and out of her.

"We look...good...together," she panted softly.

"We look so fucking good together," he rasped. He gazed back up at her face. "You're so damned beautiful."

She smiled, beckoning Caden to kiss her. He released her leg and lowered himself back onto his elbows, then cupped his hands under her shoulders for leverage. He claimed her mouth until their need to breathe made it too hard to continue.

The room filled with the sounds of their lovemaking. The shifting of bodies moving together. Their panting breaths and impassioned moans. Every single sound reverberated directly to his cock and made him want her even more.

Enjoying the closeness of their bodies, Caden hunched himself possessively over her and slammed into her again and again. He rolled his pelvic bone into her clit with each thrust. The sound of her whimpering when he hit it spot on was the best reward.

"Sweet Caden," she whispered as she pressed a few open-mouthed kisses to his yellow rose. He lowered his head and reverently kissed her forehead.

When she wrapped her legs around him, the added depth tightened everything in his groin. "Fuck," he said through a dry swallow, "I want you...to come again. Can you do that for me?" he panted.

"Close," she rasped.

"Touch yourself. Come with me."

She groaned and reached down with her right hand. Her hand swiped down to the wetness he was bringing out of her. She separated her fingers into a V and slid them around him as he plunged in and out of her. "Aw, Christ." The added sensation shoved him closer to the edge. "*Red*," he cautioned, his voice a raw scrape.

Her fingers moved, then circled over her clit. He lifted up just a little and glanced down. But he had to look away before the incredible sight of her touching herself did him in before she was ready.

"Just feel. Feel me filling you up. Feel your fingers stroking yourself."

A pleading whimper erupted from her throat. "Keep talking, Caden."

He moaned. The strain of holding back his orgasm flared. Then he blurted out the feeling most driving him crazy in that moment. "You're so tight, and it's so fucking good. Everything about you..."

He felt her tighten around his cock and he groaned. *Just a little more. Push her a little more.*

"Come," he growled through clenched teeth, "come on me."

The hand on his back clenched. Her short fingernails pinched as they sank into his skin.

"Mak—"

"Coming! Oh God!"

"Fuck, yes." Her orgasm roared through her. Her inner walls milked at him relentlessly. It was all he could take. "Oh, Christ." He thrust into her once, twice, a third time. His release erupted into her still-clenching depths. His muscles strained as the most intense orgasm of his life slammed through him. He stilled himself all the way in her and shuddered against her as his cock continued to twitch. "Makenna," he whispered as he panted into her soft wavy hair. He pressed kisses down onto the damp skin of her forehead, then allowed his head to fall into the crook of her neck when he gently pulled out of her.

Long, comfortable moments of blissful silence passed. Being with her had been incredible, but it was how at ease he felt with her that most had him hoping he could stay the night, and tomorrow, and the month...

Peace was not an emotion with which he was much familiar, but with Makenna, he had it. And he didn't know how he'd ever give it up.

CHAPTER NINE

Makenna was speechless. She'd guessed earlier in the evening Caden would prove an attentive lover, but she wasn't prepared for just how well he anticipated her needs, sometimes before she did herself, and how he made sure every one of them was fulfilled. It was a heady thing, being the center of someone else's efforts and attention. She felt giddy.

And he'd felt so good in her. He was the most well-endowed man she'd ever been with, and *Holy cow!* the pleasure she got from the sensation of fullness alone would've made the sex great. But the way he moved his body, the way he rolled his hips, the way his hands possessed her, the reflexive sweet kisses he dropped all over her—it all felt effortless, natural, with him, which was why she'd been able to orgasm again. She'd never before been able to come again so quickly after orgasming. But Caden had drawn it out of her with his body, his words, the deep need in his voice for her to join him when he fell.

Most of all, he'd made her feel desirable, beautiful, sexy. These feelings enabled her to be completely free with him.

She stroked light trailing fingertips over his back where he had collapsed on top of her. She wriggled a little and turned her head to kiss his stubbled cheek.

He lifted up from her neck and smiled at her, then pressed a series of soft, worshipful kisses against her lips. "You doing okay?"

She smiled. "I'm mighty fine."

His smile turned into a grin. "Yes, you are."

She gave him a quick peck. "You want something to drink?" she asked. "I have to get up to go to the bathroom anyway."

"Yeah, sounds good." He rolled off to her side and ran his fingertips from her neck down to her belly button. She squirmed, every part of her body now completely over sensitized from the immense pleasure he'd given her.

Makenna scooted off the bed and glanced back at him. He wasn't even trying to pretend he wasn't watching her nakedness stroll around the room. She smirked, knowing full well she'd be doing the same thing to him.

"You can use the bathroom in there if you want, I'll use the one out here."

He propped himself up on an elbow and gave her a very purposeful once-over. "Okay."

She shook her head and walked out of the room, chuckling.

After cleaning up in the hall bathroom, Makenna made her way back to the kitchen and smiled at the almost-dinner they'd made. She quickly returned all the ingredients back to the fridge, deciding she'd rethink whether everything ought to be thrown out when she had more brain power in the morning. Then she settled all the dirty dishes in the sink.

She scooped up the clothes they'd shed and piled them on the counter. Smiling, she pulled Caden's black shirt out and slipped it over her head. It was miles too big on her, but it felt great. She giggled like a school girl at the thought of his reaction.

She set a small tray on the counter and loaded it up with two bottles of water, some orange juice for her and a fresh can of Coke for him, and a big bunch of cold green grapes. She carried the lot of it into her room and found he'd switched on the lamp on her nightstand. He'd slipped his boxers and jeans back on and sat propped up against her headboard, his long legs stretched out in front of him.

"Nice shirt." He smirked at her, but his eyes smoldered.

"I thought so." She winked at him as she slid the tray between them and climbed up on the bed. "Help yourself."

Caden plucked a bottle of water off the tray and downed half of it in one greedy gulp. The sight of his Adam's apple bobbing in his throat made her squirm a little. She shook her head at herself as she grabbed her glass of juice and took a considerably smaller drink.

He recapped the bottle and sat forward, then broke off a stem of grapes. He threw two in his mouth and closed his eyes as he chewed.

Makenna reached down and plucked a handful off the stem. The sweet juiciness exploded in her mouth as she chewed. "Mmm. Good," she murmured.

He popped two more in his mouth and smiled. "Very."

A flash of red light behind Caden caught her eye. "Wow," she said. "It's 1:30. I had no idea." She gulped down the rest of her orange juice.

Caden glanced over his shoulder. "Um, yeah." He ate another grape and looked down at the two he was rolling around in his hand. His jaw ticked, that same way it had in the elevator when she'd first seen him.

Makenna frowned. "Hello?" He cut his eyes back up at her. "What just happened?"

His brow furrowed. "I…nothing. Really." He smiled, but it wasn't *her* smile.

Not again.

She cocked an eyebrow at him, trying to imagine what was wrong. "I call bullshit."

He chuckled and ran his hand over his scar, then sighed. "It's late."

She debated for only a second, then resolved the risk was more than worth it. Pushing the tray out of the way, she crawled over until she was kneeling in front of him. She cupped her right hand around his neck and her left hand around the back of his head, then gently tugged at him until the scarred side of his head faced her. Quite deliberately, she reached up and traced soft reverent kisses from his temple, along the scar over his ear, and all the way back to the very end of it at the hairline on his neck. She sat back on her heels and turned his face so she could see his now-flaming eyes.

Taking a deep breath, she asked, "Do you have somewhere to be?"

He shook his head.

"Because I'd like you to stay, if you want to. There wasn't any hidden meaning behind my pointing out the time. I was just surprised, just so you know."

He chuckled and nodded. "Okay. I'd like to stay."

She released a deep breath as relief and joy flooded her. "Good. And Caden?"

"Yeah?" He quirked a crooked smile.

"So there's no more weirdness or uncertainty...I like you." The warmth of a blush blossomed on her cheeks.

The smile she loved brightened his face and crinkled his eyes. "I like you, too."

Inside she was jumping up and down and screaming, "He likes me too, he likes me too!" Outside, she reached behind her and grabbed a few grapes. "Open," she said.

The dimples deepened on his face as his smile grew. He opened his mouth. She popped one grape in his mouth and two in her own, trying to suppress a smile while she chewed.

Then she thought for a moment. She wanted to know more about him—she wanted to know everything. So she sat back and looked at him, finally drawing her finger around the outline of his yellow rose tattoo.

"Tell me about this?"

❧❧❧

After Makenna left to get them something to drink, Caden had cleaned up and gotten dressed, not sure what to expect, or whether to expect anything. He knew what he wanted. He wanted to stay the night. He wanted to fall asleep holding her. Not once in the last fourteen years had he felt as comfortable with another woman, as accepted. And they'd been so damned good together. All night long, everything had felt so natural with her. Now that he'd found that, found *her*, he wanted everything she'd give him.

And then she'd returned wearing his shirt. The black of it highlighted the contrasting pale porcelain of her legs and the fiery hue of her loose curls. Somehow, his body had found some last reserve of energy, because the sight of her in his clothes made his cock stir again. If he got the chance, he was going to give her his Station Seven baseball jersey with his name silk-screened on the back.

He'd been savoring the image of her wearing a shirt that would mark her as his when she'd pointed out the time. The air had left his lungs. *My time's finally up*, was all he could think. His gut clenched with unreasonable disappointment.

She'd noticed and called him on his shit—as she'd been doing all night. And he...loved her for it. *Yeah, I'm not even going to pretend it's something else.* Because, just then, as she kissed him—*kissed his scar*—and told him she liked him and pulled him back from the edge of a downward spiral, he thought he just might be in love with Makenna James.

Her finger tickled the outline of his rose. He told her its simple story. "My mom had a rose garden. Yellow was her favorite." He grabbed her hand and brought it to his lips.

Makenna pulled her hand free and pointed to the red cross on his upper bicep. "And this one?"

"It's the badge from my station."

She raked her fingernails over his left side. He flinched and swatted at her hand, making her laugh. "And this one?" she asked as she nudged him to sit forward so she could trace the big abstract tribal around to his back.

Something about her intense exploration of his ink felt incredibly intimate to him, but he just shrugged. "No story behind that one, really. I just liked it. And it took a long time to do."

She crawled in to kneel behind him. Her knees settled against the outside of his hips and her warmth radiated against his back.

He sucked in a breath and shivered when she pressed four kisses against the large Old English lettering on his right shoulder—the tattoo of Sean's name. It had been his very first tattoo—he'd lied about his age and used a fake ID to get it done on the day Sean would've turned fifteen. His chest felt full and tight at the same time, but above it all he admired and appreciated the way Makenna met his issues head on—kissing his scar, comforting him about the loss of his family, making him feel so accepted by wanting to understand why he'd marked himself again and again.

He anticipated her fingers before they fell on the lettering on his left shoulder. "What does this say?" She traced over the four traditional Chinese characters he'd had done on the fifth anniversary of the accident.

"It says 'never forget.' "

She kneaded his shoulder muscles, and he groaned and tilted his head forward. Her hands were surprisingly strong for being so small. After a while, her thumbs worked deep circles down either side of his spine until she reached the back of his jeans.

When she wrapped her arms around him and hugged, laying her cheek on his shoulder, he sank back into her embrace. It was an unusually peaceful moment for him. He felt so cared for. They sat that way for several long, comfortable minutes.

"Got any others?" she eventually asked.

He wrapped his arms over hers. "Another tribal on my calf. Wanna see?"

She nodded against his shoulder, then dropped her arms as he leaned forward and pulled up the leg to his jeans as far as he could. The black lines curved up and down the outside of his leg like feathers, or blades.

"Does it hurt?" she asked as she went back to massaging his back.

"It can. Some places more than others."

"Is that why you do it?"

He spun to the right and dropped his legs to the floor, his upper body twisting further around so he could search her face.

Despite being surprised at the abruptness of his movement, she leaned forward to kiss him. "Caden, I like your tattoos. I mean"—she paused and blushed beautifully—"I *really* like them. It's just…"

"Just what?"

"They hurt. And you said you got this one"—she stroked his left side—"because it took a long time to do. And the dragon was part of proving to yourself you'd beaten your fear."

He nodded, studying her face intently. She was choosing her words carefully. He could almost see her thoughts playing out on her face, a face he was learning to read better and better. A face he found so very lovely.

"I think—" She dropped her hands in her lap again and flashed her baby blues at him. "Well, it's like they're your armor."

Caden's jaw dropped. He didn't know what to say, because never, ever had he thought of all his ink that way. Instead, he'd thought of them as a way to remember, he'd thought of them as a form of penance, and he'd not minded, after a certain point, that they might keep people away. But he'd never specifically thought of them as offering him protection. But she was right. They allowed him to control the pain he felt—both physical and emotional—something that had been taken from him on that long-ago summer night.

Her observation was so in tune with who he was and what had happened to him he felt ready to turn over some of that control, to entrust *her* with some of it.

He lunged at her and tackled her against the headboard with the force of his kiss. He swallowed her surprised gasp as he pushed his tongue into her mouth, now tasting of the sweetness of grapes and oranges.

When he pulled back she was laughing and smiling. Her eyes scanned over his face. "These are sexy as hell, too," she said, fingering his lip and brow piercings.

He threw his head back and laughed. Her timing was perfect. She had a knack for injecting humor in serious conversations just when it was needed. Her giggle warmed him. He leaned forward again and kissed her, scraping his bottom lip over hers to make sure she felt his spider bites. She whimpered and he grinned. After a few moments he settled back against her chest again.

Minutes passed with Caden leaning sideways against Makenna's abdomen while she stroked his back and he played with the ends of her hair. "You have the prettiest hair I've ever seen, Red. And it smells fucking phenomenal."

"I knew it! I knew you sniffed my hair."

He tilted his head to look up at her, chuckling uncomfortably.

But the beaming smile on her face was all pleased. "Don't worry," she said when she saw his embarrassed expression. "I sniffed you, too. I love your aftershave."

He nodded and tucked his head back down against her. "Good to know," he said through a smile.

More comfortable minutes passed and she sighed. "I still owe you an omelet."

He chuckled. "Yeah, we kinda skipped that, didn't we?"

Her voice sounded like a smile. "Uh, yeah. I didn't mind, though." She kissed the top of his head.

"Me neither. And, anyway, I still owe you a pizza."

"Ooh, yeah." She wriggled underneath him like she was dancing. "And a movie, too."

"And a movie, too." Caden grinned where he leaned against her. She was making plans with him, plans for the future. He was fucking thrilled.

They lay together for a few more minutes, then Makenna yawned. "Let's get comfortable," she said.

Caden pushed off the bed and extended a hand to help Makenna. He picked up the tray. "I'll take this out to the kitchen."

"Thanks," she said as she pulled the covers down.

When he returned, she was lying under the comforter on the side where they'd been sitting. He came around the other side and shed his jeans before slipping under with her. "Oh, God." He chuckled. "That feels good."

She clicked off the lamp and then rolled over to him. He lifted his arm so she could fit into the nook along the side of his body. Despite the novelty of being with a woman like this, it all felt completely natural to Caden. And that made him cherish it all the more. Cherish *her* all the more.

I could get used to this, he thought as Makenna fit herself along his side and slid her knee onto his thigh. He was bone-achingly tired but happy beyond anything he'd ever imagined might be possible for him.

Just as his eyes drooped, she pressed a kiss against his collarbone and squeezed her arm across his chest. "I love...that elevator," she said.

With a sleepy smile and a full heart, he turned his head and kissed into her soft hair. "Aw, Red. I love that elevator, too."

CADEN GRAYSON INTERVIEW

[Originally posted at Sizzling Hot Books]

Interviewer: The first (and only for a long while) glimpse you had of Makenna was her red hair. You seemed to really like this and even nicknamed her Red. Are you attracted to a specific type of woman or attribute on women (legs or hair or such)?

Caden: Aw, geez, you're not even going to ease me into this interviewing thing, are ya? Truth is, I didn't get all focused on "types" and "attributes" because I figured nothing long-term was happening for me anyway. So, I've got one and only one type. Red hair like silk, blue eyes that are heaven in a stare, a trail of freckles on her…wait. Are there men reading this? Yeah, I'm done then. You get the point. Makenna is it for me.

I: You tell Makenna that you're claustrophobic. Can you tell us why?

C: Well, that shit's obvious, don't ya think? Sorry, sorry. Didn't mean to curse. It's just, from the first moment, her laughter helped me pull back from that panic attack. Focusing on her the sound of her laughter, her voice…that helped. Um, my therapist used to call it 'Stop and Replace.' Stop the anxiety-causing thoughts and replace them with something positive. So I had to tell her, because I needed her voice to focus me. And I liked talking to her. *Palms side of head.* Do we have to talk about this?

I: In the building where you meet Makenna, you tell her you are there to settle your father's estate. You don't really seem upset by his passing, unlike how you still grieve over the loss of your mother and brother. Can you tell us why the contrasting attitudes?

C: *Deep breath, long sigh. Flexes and rolls right shoulder.* After the accident happened, the man I knew as my father disappeared. There came a point when he couldn't even look at me—I took after my mother. Sean and I both did. He became quiet, angry, easily frustrated. So, my father, he died the same night we lost Mom and Sean. I'd been through mourning him years before he died, but it was different because, really, he *was* still there. And it seemed to me he made the *choice* to go away, a choice Mom and Sean never had, a choice that left me, at fourteen, without much in the way of family. So, no, I didn't feel the same about him dying. If anything, miserable as he was, he was probably better off going. Damn.

I: So, you're a paramedic. Is this linked to your guilt because of surviving the accident that killed your mother and brother?

C: Not guilt, no. Just a desire to try to ease others going through something similar. Every day I go out there, I'm saving someone else's Mom and Sean. Next question.

I: You have several tattoos and a couple of piercings. How many tats do you have?

C: Uh, seven, for now.

I: So, you'll get more?

C: Without question, but I don't know what yet.

I: What is the meaning behind each of them?

C: Well, um, the badge on my right bicep's pretty self-explanatory—that's for my fire station in Fairlington. The dragon on my right hand and forearm, like I told Makenna, I thought of that as my fear, and putting it on my arm was me, taming it. Sean's name on my right shoulder, again, self-explanatory, and the characters for 'Never Forget' on my left shoulder are, too. Let's see…oh, right, the big wrap-around tribal on my torso, I just liked that because it was cool. And it took a long time to do, which was a plus, then. The yellow rose on my chest was for my mom—they were her favorite flower, and she grew them in her garden. And, uh, I've got another tribal on my calf. Just because.

I: Do you think Makenna would ever get a tattoo? Have you two talked about that?

C: *Lips slide into a sexy smile*. She's thought about it and we have talked about it. Decision's totally hers and I'd support her either way. She doesn't need to do a single thing to be anymore appealing to me, though. That's for damn sure.

I: Why the piercings?

C: Thought they looked cool. And they hurt like a bitch. Uh, sorry.

I: Do they have any meaning like the tats?

C: Not really. *Flicks tongue over spider bites*.

I: Several times you refer to how you have only a few close friends, a small circle of intimates. You even think about how your scars and tats keep you isolated. Is this something you encourage? Is there a reason behind the isolation (beyond the scars and tats)?

C: I went from being your average surly teenager before the accident to an angry fuck of a teenager after. That hit just at the moment you're figuring out who the hell you are, and who I was then was kinda dark and scary and unstable. So, I withdrew. It was how my father handled his shit, and I followed suit. I got the first of the tats on what would've been Sean's fifteenth birthday. I was almost seventeen. During the hour it took to ink those Old English letters onto my shoulder, the tattoo gun was all I could think about. That was incentive enough to get more. Hell, no, I don't encourage people to deal with their shit the way I did. Just look at Makenna. She suffered loss, too, and she's one of the most outgoing, friendly, compassionate people I know. You want a role model, follow her.

I: Makenna is a strong, modern woman. You also found both of you have many things in common while talking during your time stuck in the elevator. Did she ever intimidate you? After keeping yourself isolated for so long, did you find it hard to take a chance with her?

C: Well, yeah, she did intimidate me, since I'm kind of a social misfit and all, and she's brilliant, and brave, and beautiful. Basically, all the things I'm not. I mean, shit, I started off our time in there by kicking her in the ankle. You should've seen the big purple bruise I left. Saw it the next morning and about flipped, but I made it up to her. *Rubs side of head and grins. Shakes head out of memories.* I mean, how many times did I trip up and say something totally stupid, at first? She was the one that helped me calm down so I could talk like a normal human being. You know, I didn't have a choice but to take a chance. I was trapped in a pitch-black box—my worst nightmare come to life. I *needed* her help, which meant I had to reach out and ask for it. That's not something I usually do. Had we been trapped but those lights had stayed on, well, let's just say I offer a word of thanks every day that things happened the way they did.

Hey, are we done? 'Cause I gotta pick Makenna up soon. We're going to see Hangover 2 tonight. You know how much we love stupid humor movies. Can't tell you how many times we've seen the first Hangover movie. *Grins.* Thanks for having me here.

I: Hey, Caden, one last question? Will there be any more of you and Makenna?

C: *The smile brings out his dimples.* Anything's possible. Thanks, again.

ABOUT THE AUTHOR

Laura Kaye is the New York Times and USA Today bestselling author of over a dozen books in contemporary and paranormal romance. Laura grew up amidst family lore involving angels, ghosts, and evil-eye curses, cementing her life-long fascination with storytelling and the supernatural. Laura lives in Maryland with her husband, two daughters, and cute-but-bad dog, and appreciates her view of the Chesapeake Bay every day.

Visit Laura Kaye at http://www.LauraKayeAuthor.com/
Follow Laura on Twitter at @laurakayeauthor
Like LauraKayeWrites on Facebook

ACKNOWLEDGEMENTS

As my first published book, *Hearts in Darkness* will always be special to me, and I have a lot of people to thank for supporting this story and helping make my writing dreams come true. The first thanks I must extend goes to Eilidh Mackenzie, my editor at The Wild Rose Press, which originally published the book, for believing in a story that mostly took place in the dark.

I also want to thank Tricia "Pickyme" Schmitt, the cover artist for the original and revised versions of the cover of this book. I first met Trish at the RWA conference in Orlando in July of 2010 and mentioned off the cuff that I had *no* idea what kind of cover I'd get for a story that took place mostly in the dark. She was immediately excited and encouraged me to request her to do it. Best random meet I've ever had! Our careers have developed side-by-side, and we joke all the time that she gave me a big boost with that delicious cover (and it's so true!).

Mostly, I want to thank the readers and bloggers who fell in love with Red and Good Sam and talked about it on their blogs, on Facebook, on Twitter, and with their friends. The way you all embraced this book has been one of the highlights of my writing journey so far, and I want you to know how much it means to me. You guys rock! ~LK

WANT MORE CONTEMPORARY ROMANCE FROM LAURA KAYE?

CHECK OUT:

Her Forbidden Hero (Heroes #1)

You always want what you can't have... She's always been off-limits...Former Army Special Forces Sgt. Marco Vieri has never thought of Alyssa Scott as more than his best friend's little sister, but her return home changes that...and challenges him to keep his war-borne demons at bay. Marco's not the same person he was back when he protected Alyssa from her abusive father, and he's not about to let her see the mess he's become....but now she's all grown up. When Alyssa takes a job at the bar where Marco works, her carefree smiles wreak havoc on his resolve to bury his feelings. How can he protect her when he can't stop thinking about her in his bed? But Alyssa's not looking for protection—not anymore. Now that she's back in his life, she's determined to heal her forbidden hero, one touch at a time...

One Night with a Hero (Heroes #2)

He wants just one night...After growing up with an abusive, alcoholic father, Army Special Forces Sgt. Brady Scott vowed never to marry or have kids. Sent stateside to get his head on straight—and his anger in check—Brady's looking for a distraction. He finds it in his beautiful new neighbor's one-night-only offer for hot sex, but her ability to make him forget is addictive. Suddenly, Brady's not so sure he can stay away....what they need is each other.Orphaned as a child, community center director Joss Daniels swore she'd never put herself in a position to be left behind again, but she can't deny herself one sizzling night with the sexy soldier who makes her laugh and kisses her senseless. When Joss discovers she's pregnant, Brady's rejection leaves her feeling abandoned. Now, they must overcome their fears before they lose the love and security they've found in each other, but can they let go of the past to create a future together?

ec

Five dishonored soldiers
Former Special Forces
One last mission
These are the men of Hard Ink...

Hard As It Gets (Hard Ink #1)

Tall, dark, and lethal...Trouble just walked into Nicholas Rixey's tattoo parlor. Becca Merritt is warm, sexy, wholesome—pure temptation to a very jaded Nick. He's left his military life behind to become co-owner of Hard Ink Tattoo, but Becca is his ex-commander's daughter. Loyalty won't let him turn her away. Lust has plenty to do with it too.

With her brother presumed kidnapped, Becca needs Nick. She just wasn't expecting to want him so much. As their investigation turns into all-out war with an organized crime ring, only Nick can protect her. And only Becca can heal the scars no one else sees.

Desire is the easy part. Love is as hard as it gets. Good thing Nick is always up for a challenge...

Hard As You Can (Hard Ink #2)

Ever since hard-bodied, drop-dead-charming Shane McCallan strolled into the dance club where Crystal Dean works, he's shown a knack for getting beneath her defenses. For her little sister's sake, Crystal can't get too close. Until her job and Shane's mission intersect, and he reveals talents that go deeper than she could have guessed.

Shane McCallan doesn't turn his back on a friend in need, especially a former Special Forces teammate running a dangerous, off-the-books operation. Nor can he walk away from Crystal. The gorgeous blonde waitress is hiding secrets she doesn't want him to uncover. Too bad. He's exactly the man she needs to protect her sister, her life, and her heart. All he has to do is convince her that when something feels this good, you hold on as hard as you can—and never let go.

Made in the USA
San Bernardino, CA
12 August 2015